A LONG BLUE MONDAY

A
LONG BLUE
MONDAY

Erhard von Büren

Matador
9 Priory Business Park,
Wistow Road, Kibworth Beauchamp,
Leicestershire. LE8 0RX
Tel: 0116 279 2299
Email: books@troubador.co.uk
Web: www.troubador.co.uk/matador
Twitter: @matadorbooks

ISBN 978 1789014 174

British Library Cataloguing in Publication Data.
A catalogue record for this book is available from the British Library.

Printed and bound by CPI Group (UK) Ltd, Croydon, CR0 4YY
Typeset in 11pt Aldine401 BT by Troubador Publishing Ltd, Leicester, UK

Matador is an imprint of Troubador Publishing Ltd

CONTENTS

I

THAT SUMMER –
PROLOGUE

'For days sometimes he did nothing but lie half asleep in the shade of a bush on the river bank.'

Sherwood Anderson, *Poor White*

Three or four times a day, I'd walk along Haselweg as far as the reservoir, a grass-covered mound up near the crossing; I'd turn left down the steep field path to the wood, then skirt the wood as far as the corner above Langendorf; from there I'd take the dirt track between two fields to reach the road that goes up the slope and across to Sagacker Heights.

I remember the heat in June – it was in the June heat that those daily walks began. I remember the July heat, the heat even early in the morning. I remember the peal of bells down from Oberdorf parish church, the eleven o'clock chimes up from the town – Langendorf didn't have a church of its own yet, the chimes, many-voiced and distant, came up from the town.

It was in the summer of nineteen fifty-nine, my third year at the teacher training college.

I remember striding along the edge of the wood, along the edge of the wheatfields, outwardly calm, full of turmoil inside. A jumble of words and sentences ran wildly through my head, snatches of conversation, things I'd overheard, things I'd invented: What does someone like Claudia say to someone like Bede? What does she say to someone like me? What did she say? What might she have said? What shall I make her say? Beginnings of conversations, fragments of dialogue in varying settings.

A play had to be written. Already in May I'd spent every free afternoon and every evening writing plots. For weeks, college had been no more than a distraction.

In the second week of June I decided to stay at home. If I continued to go to school I'd never finish the play. The play had to be written. Somehow or other I had to get out of this whole affair.

The solution had come to me in an allotment up on the Zurichberg. On Ascension Thursday I'd hitched a lift to Zurich and seen Thornton Wilder's *The Skin of Our Teeth* at the Schauspielhaus. After the performance I looked for a spot to spend the night.

In an allotment at the top end of Hadlaubsteig I found a roofed porch with a bench. I found the porch and the bench, but I didn't find sleep. I felt cold, and as I gazed, freezing, across the moonlight-drenched bushes and vegetable patches, the hut roofs and the water butts, I suddenly knew what I had to do.

Dawn had not yet broken when I left the garden and went down to the town. There was only one thing to be done, but it was a big thing and I had to get started.

Bahnhofplatz, Bellevueplatz, there and back and there again, through the Niederdorf district, or along Bahnhofstrasse. At the Sankt Annahof store I bought a stiff-covered exercise book and started to write down all the things that had to be included in the play.

Even finding the right title was no easy matter. I kept thinking of all those superb American titles: *Cat on a Hot Tin Roof, The Crucible, A Streetcar Named Desire.* I couldn't think of anything that was even half as meaningful and at the same time so enthrallingly vivid. All the impediments and frustrations in my life had to go into the title, but also defiance, pride, hope and passion – everything had to be in it.

That Friday in Zurich something else dawned on me: writing just one play for Claudia wouldn't do. It had to be three plays, something on the scale of the trilogy *Mourning Becomes Electra* at the very least. And they would all put in an appearance, albeit with other names: down in the town, Claudia and Elizabeth and Bede and Corinne and Conrad and Jacob, the whole gang; and up in the village, the Ganters in their house by the stream: my father, my mother, my younger sister, my elder sister. I'd put them all in it, I still didn't know how, but I'd have to find a way soon.

In the evening I went to the cinema. I spent the rest of that Friday night on a bench by the lake.

The model pupil playing truant for two days – it was a premiere. No, it was only the dress rehearsal for the big truancy that lay ahead.

The summer of fifty-nine, three weeks in June and two weeks in July and then the whole of the holidays.

Even when I wasn't sitting in front of my typewriter I kept at it. If I went outside the house or down to the stream I took my exercise book and pencil with me.

I still see the pencilled writing, the long loops and tails, I see the haste in which it was written – in the kitchen, in front of the house, on the bench beside the old chicken hut down by the stream. Not a moment to be lost, not a single idea should be lost, the trilogy had to be written, I had to come to an end, the thing had to be brought to an end.

I often worked on the landing. I placed the small table against the staircase balustrade, up in the front near the window. When I looked up from my typewriter I saw the ash trees over by the stream. With the window open I could hear the regular murmur of the stream, the rising, falling murmur of the ash trees. I saw the wind blowing through the tangled leaves: the branches bent, sprang back, bent again, the leaves glistened whitish, ruffled and tossed around by the gusts.

Out on the landing by the window was my favourite place. In the afternoon no one ever disturbed me. In the afternoon, my mother was away too. That summer, she was working part time in a shirt factory in Langendorf.

I might have guessed that the three ringbinders, the two folders and the stiff-covered exercise books would still be lying around somewhere. On leaving home, in the autumn of that year, I'd left everything behind.

I hadn't burned the exercise books and the files. In my view that would have been just too theatrical. I'd simply left them where they were, in a box up in the attic, together with a couple of other boxes full of old books. I seldom threw anything away, but I also hardly ever deliberately and carefully stored anything.

So I must always have known that those things would still be lying around somewhere. And I could also always have said more or less what was filed away in those folders and ringbinders: the drafts, the fair copy. I'd probably also have been able to name the titles of the different parts: 'On the Wall', 'Chaconne', 'Blue Monday'. And hadn't I, toward the end of the holidays, named the whole thing 'A Long Blue Monday'? Inspired by Eugene O'Neill's *Long Day's Journey into Night*? Finally I'd had to hurry: Before the end of the holidays, and before school started again – started for me too, after all that truancy – I'd wanted to go to Zurich once more, freed of the burden, freed of constraints. As a reward for having freed myself of the constraints and the burden.

A long blue Monday, yes that's probably what it had been.

And here's something else I could have recalled at any time these past forty years – if I'd really wanted to:

The hero is sitting on the Carrels' garden wall by the river Aare. That is, he's sitting at the very front of the stage, his legs dangling over the apron, the way you might dangle your legs over a wall, and he talks and talks, without looking at the audience, his gaze directed over their heads to the Carrels' house. Back there – in the dim light between the ceiling and the heads of the audience – there's nothing to be seen, unfortunately, except for a couple of brightly lit windows: there's no Claudia there, ready to come out onto the balcony and lean over the railing, all ears for what the young man down on the wall has to say.

Behind him on the stage, however, domestic battle scenes are being enacted, plenty to be seen there: the family show, the payday pub-crawl, naturalistic dialogues in the house by the stream till long past midnight, the same as ever, being shown now, while the son of this same family, seated here on the wall, addresses his soliloquies to the auditorium, over the heads of the audience, his eyes on the imaginary windows of the Carrel villa. Behind him on the proscenium stage, the burden of the past; in front of him, up in the air, the dream of a splendid future; and in between, from the stage apron to the audience, the soliloquies of the anti-hero. The house by the stream and the house on the Aare and the wall in between.

I simply fitted in everything I'd ever seen at the municipal theatre and at the four cinemas of the town when screen adaptations of plays by Tennessee Williams and Eugene O'Neill were shown. I tried to fit in everything I'd ever read in the paperback editions of modern plays about stage settings and stage directions: 'viewing from the walls', slide projections, memory sequences and dream scenes behind gauze curtains; along with a stage manager, and an author who is on stage from time to time and starts arguments with the stage manager, people in the audience who start acting, and actors who go and sit down in the audience. I used every means available to air my personal drama, and to do so to the greatest effect.

Filed away in three ring binders: that much I always knew. Enough, at all events, to deter me from ever wanting to take another look. It wouldn't have bothered me in the least if the files had landed in the waste paper collection or in the dustbin.

In all those years I'd never ever given a thought to what exactly I'd written at the time. But the fact that I'd written something, the circumstances in which I'd done so, how I'd gone about it: that's what I remembered.

A model pupil gone astray. But why oh why was I secretly pleased about it?

'Student digs for a retired English teacher,' says Anna. 'Not bad at all, I almost envy you. Internet connection, even a kitchen. And everything so beautifully tidy, and the bookshelves still almost empty. Actually, that's something that does rather surprise me.'

The way grown-up daughters make fun of their fathers. But isn't it nice of her to have come by?

She's been working in a hospital in Biel since February, and when she goes to Zurich to see her boyfriend she occasionally stops off here. Her third job as a house officer. Or is it the fourth? There's no need to worry about Anna. Competent like Erica, her mother.

'So you think you'll get on faster with your Anderson here,' says Anna.

'I hope so,' I say.

'But that can't be the only reason why you moved out of Winznau!'

'What other reasons might there have been?'

'Erica? Doesn't she have anything to do with it?'

'Well, she doesn't have any objections. On the contrary. She thinks it's really useful for her to have a pied-à-terre here. Of course, if the pied-à-terre was in Paris or London or Edinburgh she'd get more out of it. But Solothurn's not bad either.'

Anna laughs.

'The flat was offered to me, I wasn't specially looking for anything. I don't know how long I can stay. Perhaps up until the autumn. It's only temporary.'

It's all been for nothing, all in vain, a life wasted. How lightly that now passes through my mind! It's as though it had nothing to do with me. It doesn't make me feel depressed, it doesn't bother me.

It's contrary to all psychiatric experience, this feeling of elation early in the morning. A mood if not depressed, at least subdued. Listlessness. Nothing gets done in the morning, in the morning everything seems difficult.

But I myself feel light in the morning, lighter than at any other time of day. I awake easily from a light sleep, I drink weak coffee, I don't worry about anything, I don't worry about my new ailments, I don't worry about past annoyances. I sit in the kitchen, watch the day break, see the pale light in the sky grow brighter and brighter. I see the sickle moon above the roof ridge of the house next door, hear the crescendo of the traffic in the distance. I feel light, I am light. Not that I feel exactly full of drive, but I don't feel tired either. This early-morning euphoria, Anna assured me, goes against all received psychiatric opinion.

Is it a consequence of that long-forgotten time when I was still a model pupil and willed myself to get up before six every morning? Of course I didn't always manage, despite all my efforts. The good habit was rather weak.

These days I don't have to make an effort, it's more or less automatic. And at the kitchen table, my mind comes up with half sentences like: all for nothing, all in vain, nothing I wanted to do accomplished – which seems to me to be true for the day before, for the week before, indeed for ever.

It was as if, in the stillness of the morning, I took real pleasure in listing all the things that hadn't worked out for me. Defeat upon defeat and, in the other column, a couple of narrow victories, wins on points. A model schoolboy only ever wins on points. If indeed there's anything like victory and defeat. In the end it probably comes to the same thing, in the end it comes to a draw.

And the Chinese man in the 'Song of the Earth' comes to mind. Or did I find the story somewhere else? The old man who retires to the foot of a mountain. Without bitterness, he leaves human society. It's summer, the nights are hot. Towards morning a shower of rain refreshes him. A fine mist lies in the ravine. The sun rises. A blackbird calls out into the stillness.

Whatever my thoughts, I enjoy the morning, I enjoy the lightness within me, the lightness around me.

Or am I only glad that I don't have to pack my briefcase anymore?

I really must have started to hate it! Getting up effortlessly in the morning had long become a thing of the past. I was often in a bad mood, especially in the early morning. I saw the day ahead, the classes of young people in front of me. Youth has something invigorating, oh yes, definitely – but classrooms full, a whole building full!

I was right to stop. It wasn't high time, not quite that, it was time, that's all.

II

Claudia – Shadow Play

'There also I meet myself and recall myself – what, when, or where I did a thing, and how I felt when I did it.'

Aurelius Augustinus, *Confessions*

1

Revox – Bird Songs

Choruses of birdsong. Claudia's father had recorded them with his tape recorder, in the garden, every Saturday morning from March to September. Now it was on, from the left spool over the recording head to the right spool, smaller and smaller but faster and faster on the left, slowing but growing on the right, and the loudspeaker recreated the summer, the garden, with twitterings and chirrupings, with warbling and tweeting. The tape recorder, the rotation, slowing down here, speeding up there, mesmerising.

That's what I remember. And not only the sound of the birds, not only the tape recorder – a Revox, the best recorder available at the time. Listening to the birdsong was probably only a diversionary tactic anyway. There, close by, lay Claudia, slim on the couch, the Revox on a stool between her and me.

'I'm sure I've had to listen to that at least ten times since last autumn,' she said, 'whenever we had visitors to dinner.' Heels and calves in silky nylon on the rough warp of the couch cover, chin propped up in her palms. 'He pieced it together from dozens of tapes,' she said. 'No wonder he's so crazy about it and wants to play it to everyone. And he tells everyone what microphones he used, he reveals all the tricks it takes to make such good separate recordings out of a medley of warblings.'

She seemed to be distancing herself, yet she also seemed pleased that I showed an interest in the technology. All that warbling and trilling played to a music-loving audience between the dessert and the house concert. What did Carrel, the engineer, want to prove? That it was purely out of the kindness of his heart that he recorded all the other things with his machine – all those duets, trios and quartets? That, as far as his wife's musical activities here in this house were concerned, all that interested him was the perfection of the recordings?

What could I know? I might have heard one or two things, a remark by Bede, a question from Elizabeth. But wasn't making fun of your parents from time to time just part of it all? Bede did it, Elizabeth did it, therefore Claudia could do it too.

She'd played me those bird songs the spring before that summer. Very early spring, it was still almost winter, the end of February perhaps, or early March, nineteen fifty-nine. About the same time the year before I still didn't know Claudia, I only knew Corinne, her schoolfriend. Corinne Weibel used to sit diagonally in front of me in the sixth year of primary school in Oberdorf, before she went on to the Gymnasium down in town. And later on, when I was also at the Kantonsschule I occasionally bumped into her. Not that we ever talked for long, we just said hello.

Shortly before the summer holidays, during my second year at training college, in a break, a girl came across the lawn from the side wing and made straight for me. 'Corinne told me that in Oberdorf you used to act in plays, at school and elsewhere too,' she said. 'We could do with an extra man. If you'd like to join us.'

That was Claudia, I'd seen her a couple of times together with Corinne. Although the Gymnasium and the training college were in the same building we hardly knew each other, and I'd never have thought that Gymnasium pupils rehearsing a play in their spare time might ask a training college student to join them.

Bede's father, a doctor in the town, had recently bought a tumbledown farmhouse. The house stood in a clearing in the wood above Rüttenen. And it was there – in Papa's dacha, as Bede called it – in the first week of the holidays, that the rehearsals were to take place. There was even talk of a real performance. The school hall would be available. That had already been settled.

The tape recorder, the revolving spools, the birdsong. Why did that particular scene remain in my memory? Claudia on the couch, I in the armchair, and between us, on the stool, the Revox recorder.

Claudia playing me her father's recordings and making derisive comments about them must have seemed like a sign, the hint of a promise that it might turn into a real love affair after all.

For me, of course, it had long been a love affair. It had been that right from the beginning, ever since the rehearsals the previous summer, since that week in the forest clearing with Corinne and Claudia, Bede and the others.

How long it is since I last thought about it! Not that I'd forgotten, no, but it was so far away, had receded further and further away, it had hardly ever had anything to do with the present, with Erica, my studies, the two children, with my work and all those things. You got over all that nonsense ages ago, I'd probably have thought, if I'd ever thought about it. But I never did think about it. I was busy with everything else, always busy with more important things.

And now? What about now? Why have I started to think about it, forty years on – more than forty years on? What makes those distant things so near again? Am I pursuing them or are they pursuing me? I catch myself paying attention when something from those times happens to cross my mind. And then I pursue the matter in my head, even try to recall everything I can remember about what it was like in the house by the stream. And what it was like in that other house, the Carrels' house, on the Aare.

2
Bede – Rehearsals in Lee Forest

In the eyes of Claudia, Conrad or Elizabeth I might – to their amazement – have been Bede's friend. Wide-eyed listener, faithful little dog in front of the loudspeaker was probably more like it. And in return, I'd occasionally assist him at the Aare wall, help him disgorge unwholesome quantities of beer as rapidly as possible. I had experience with drunkards, Bede would never be a drunkard.

To say that we were friends would have been an exaggeration. We both knew Claudia, that's all. Later on, if we chanced to meet, the same question en passant, either from him or from me, from me more often than from him: 'Heard anything from Claudia?' A regretful shrug. Talk about old friends, as there was nothing else to be said.

The glade in Lee Forest above Rüttenen. Two well-watered meadows, and a house with a low-hanging hip roof, the front facing the sun and the meadows, in the rear, a peak roof projecting above the hayloft door; the garden surrounded by a thick growth of gooseberry and currant bushes; an empty chicken pen with a coarse-meshed wire fence; plum, apple and cherry trees along the track that emerges from the wood at the lower end of the glade and, after making a broad right-hand curve at the height of the loft entry, leads back to the wood and on up the mountain.

The second week in July. In the afternoon, the coolest place was on the tiled stove. In the greenish half-light behind half-closed shutters, five voices were rehearsing a conspiracy. Bede's voice dry and resolute, Conrad's halting voice reading out orders, Elizabeth's soft soprano voice, Corinne's whispered prompts, and Claudia's voice, surprisingly rough, coming from such a narrow face. He who makes bombs must hate, must know no pity. He who is moved by higher purposes to command must be just, insensitive, cold. He who is to throw the bomb has to anticipate his fear – from the paralysing anxiety to the trembling – so that when it

19

comes to throwing the bomb the fright will be behind him, overcome. Albert Camus, *The Just Assassins*.

During our breaks, Bede lectured us on the historical background: the situation of the peasants, the situation of the petty bourgeoisie, of the middle, lower and higher grade civil servants, of the aristocracy, the situation of the secret cells, Siberian cabbage soup, the relationship between power and absolute poverty, straight and roundabout roads to revolution; Lenin had continually changed his plans, Krupskaya her purple stockings.

In the morning we learned Camus' texts by heart, separating off into the house, the barn or the orchard. Toward eleven, two people took their turn at cooking. 'Eating is at the foundation of everything,' said Bede. 'I supply the kitchen and the water. Others can do the cooking.'

After two days I knew my lines by heart and began to show the others how to act. I stood around, gesticulated, held my head stiffly, the way they stood around, gesticulated, held their heads: perhaps it could be done differently, it was only a suggestion. Someone who's ruminating sits in his chair like this, stares out in front of him like this, or like this; and someone who's trying to control his rage grips the edge of the table like this, if there's a table there; a man who's afraid but doesn't want to talk about it will beat about the bush, and it'll sound like this. I managed the demonstration-imitation with a minimum of words. All Bede had to do was say yes.

They accepted my help. Wasn't I the one who'd already had the experience of acting in several plays? Just the person they needed.

And what else could I be used for?

I'd always envied schoolmates who could entertain others, who had the ability to speak spontaneously about anything and everything. I could hardly ever think of anything suitable offhand. I could only speak more or less smoothly when I'd prepared what I was going to say in advance.

It had begun with the poems under the Christmas tree, and had continued at school. For a long time I could only attract attention by reciting poetry – in a loud clear voice that no one would have expected from the normally silent pupil. On top of that I attracted attention because I was capable of memorising entire pages of our primer and never got stuck when I was standing up by my desk or even in front of the class. Where others stuttered, stumbled or droned, I took the time to draw breath: it was nice for me to be able to speak too for once.

Every year before Christmas, a play was performed. In class three, I was the spokesman for the shepherds. The following year, I raged as Herod. The year after that, they gave me the role of the narrator: as a grandfather, I held in my left hand a long-stemmed pipe at which I took mighty puffs whenever the others had their turn to speak; a dozen grandchildren, seated around me in a semicircle, listened to the sacred story – from the census via the search for an inn in Bethlehem to the flight into Egypt; simultaneously, everything I recounted was acted out behind a tautly stretched screen so that in front of the screen in the classroom it appeared as a shadow play.

No, Bede had no reason to be embarrassed. Acting was the only way I could make myself useful here in the

21

Lee Forest glade. It would never have occurred to me to put myself forward. Nevertheless, in the end he must have got tired of doing nothing but supply commentaries. Although they'd been planned and were set for the last week of the holidays, no further rehearsals took place. Nor later on either. Some attempts were made, but there was always someone who couldn't come.

Bede's role as a stage director remained a short interlude. He soon went back to walking around with a Nietzsche or Freud paperback in his hand, supplying whoever came his way with his little phrases. 'I read so as not to think for myself.' – 'People who make good resolutions are purposely making themselves discontented.' – 'The nibbling worm shows the apple is ripe.' – 'Every woman is a cul-de-sac. If you're running a race with a woman, take something for cramps.'

He only ever proffered very few such remarks, but he always seemed to have a large supply in stock. He particularly liked dropping them when they were out of place, and he delivered them with such conviction that you could have thought he was being serious.

'Of course,' he said, 'I had a first-class upbringing. Be a good boy, come on now, get on with it! Oh yes, very nice, you're a good boy! When I sat down on the potty there was sure to be someone beside me to help – the au-pair, Mama, or even Papa himself. As a gut doctor he must have been aware of the importance of his only son's first products. And so you gave them what you could, hard work is never enjoyable, but if the spectators show their approval by continually patting your little cheeks, you can't avoid giving them something in return. What little Bede once learned, Bede never forgets. And now, make a little sentence out of it, come on, a complete one. There you are! Single words, a yes or a no, that's not enough for them. It always has to be something solid, complete, well-rounded. I took it to heart. I can't do anything else. And now if they don't like it they've only themselves to blame.'

During the following two weeks of the summer holidays I worked as a labourer on a building site, for Fröhlicher & Co. But whilst picking and shoveling and pushing wheelbarrows, I remained in the Lee Forest glade, still sitting there on the refreshingly cool tiled stove, still in St Petersburg in an attic room with conspirators. Bede was still striding around in the dim living room. Down in the ravine at the foot of the cliff he read out quotations from his paperback. He prodded between the rocks for Jura vipers. He pointed up to the buzzard that was circling in the air above the pine trees. And then, Conrad's escape from the heat into the fountain trough. Elizabeth suggested a trip to the swimming pool; but we made do with footbaths in the stream and showers under the garden hose. A farmer from Rüttenen came to mow the meadows. Cherries direct from the tree, and redcurrant desserts in abundance.

'When the Lord distributed mouths and there was a great rush I called out "here, here" at least a dozen times.' Bede liked admitting things like that. He bombarded the girls with compliments, occasionally with well-aimed jibes. No one seemed to hold it against him. Claudia, Elizabeth and he were classmates, they'd known each other for a long time. Conrad and he were in the same students' society, Corinne had been friends with Claudia ever since the Weibels had moved from Oberdorf to the town.

My stagefright only left me during the rehearsals. Whilst the others needed advice on how to act on stage, it was before and after rehearsals that I could have done with advice.

3

The House on the Aare River

In the telephone directory there was only one Carrel, so it had to be Claudia's father. He was an electrical engineer, but I knew that already. He was married to a von Matt and they lived in Römerstrasse. The von Matts were clearly an old-established family in the town: according to the directory there was a judge of that name, and also a law company, and a doctor and a businessman.

Along the road, a low wall surmounted by a white-painted wooden fence as high as your head, dense shrubbery behind. On the garden gate, a 'No hawkers' notice; an enamelled eye warned that everything was under the protection of 'Securitas'. Best to walk past quickly and turn off left down to the river bank. Here there was a fence of rusty wire netting held by iron posts and jutting out about one and a half metres into the river: private, no trespassing. Through the gaps in the bushes the gleam of the manicured lawn, a stretch of gravel path, the gleam of birch trunks. Outside on the riverbank, under the willow thicket and the ash trees, the kinds of weeds that grow in damp places.

I left my bicycle under the railway bridge. On arriving here on foot I sometimes heard voices coming from the house. We'd enjoyed sunny summer weather every day since the beginning of July and, unless a thunderstorm from the mountain broke out over the town, people stayed outdoors till late at night.

A two-storey villa with a steeply ridged roof, attic windows on the Aare side. On the town side, at right angles to the building, an extension with a big roof terrace.

Not much could be made out clearly through the foliage of the bushes and beyond the lawn, the gravel and the rose bushes. A roller shutter squeaked. Wooden sandals clattered. Glasses tinkled. Someone said something, someone else answered, a third voice joined in, a sudden rustle of leaves and I couldn't make out if the voice was male or female. The wind in the bushes and the trees, the crickets in the grass, the gurgling water: too much background noise, although I had my ears pricked up.

Nevertheless I stayed by the fence. If I went away I came back again. I remained standing there and I didn't know why I'd come. Taking every voice for Claudia's. Stepping behind the willows when headlights up on the road moved through the twilight; Römerstrasse was a road where cars seldom drove by.

Tired from looking where nothing much could be seen in the dim light, I finally retreated back to the railway bridge. How peacefully the River Aare flowed!

How still the reflection of the lights in the water! Across the river the silhouette of the Crooked Tower, the walls of the redoubt.

Through the town once more and then home. Before that summer, I'd always chosen the shortest way – Amthausplatz, Pflug, Autophon, Weissensteinstrasse – and even on the steep road through Langendorf I never dismounted from my bicycle. Now I was in no hurry, once more I took the roundabout way via the swimming pool, made detours through the Brühl, the Allmend and the Dilitsch quarters, pushed my bike even when the road wasn't steep at all.

I arrived at the house by the stream at midnight. I drank water from the tap, searched the fridge for leftovers: cold beans, rice pudding, mashed potatoes. I had to recover my strength for the following morning on the building site.

The first week of the holidays the rehearsals, then three weeks on the building site. In the last two weeks I occasionally helped out at the Furrers'. Whenever possible I went to the swimming pool.

My somnambulism was just as bad in the daytime.

The pool, the rows of cabins, the wooden sunbeds along the wall. The smell of suncream and chlorine. Swirls of dust by the 'giant stride': holding on to a chain, children ran barefoot over the gravel, leapt up with a swing of the hips, the chains clanked against the iron pole. Balls flew. People queued at the kiosk. At the horizontal bar boys hung by their knees, swung themselves up, turned somersaults.

And Bede, sitting cross-legged on the plinth of the diving board. Swallows darted about high up in the air. The wind turned the pages of his book. From time to time a shadow passed over the lawn and the pool.

'Zarathustra excuses splashes from flesh fearless enough to dive. Man, the hairless beast. Born with nothing but nakedness, that he has to cover up for the rest of his days. A chronic liar. As a gaze at your own belly button will confirm.'

He tapped the book with his fingers: 'It comes from this man here of course, another of those liars. I can't do without him: maxims plus reflections. Everything borrowed from him; with regard to women too, obviously. Just look around. It's amazing to see how assiduously suncream is being applied to what's not otherwise on display. Grill of the vanities. And at the same time they have us revolving on the spit.'

He set the book down beside the portable radio, folded his spectacles and put them in their case. 'A header's the fastest way to cool off!'

Later he came dripping across to the sunbeds.

'Look at those sun-hungry creatures, they come here in crowds in their lunch break, hoping to make their fading holiday tans last a little longer. Office girls, on their sides, on their backs, squatting, seated on their heels, or with legs stretched out, or mermaid-style. Not quite as perfect as the mannequins in shop windows, but a pretty sight all the same, don't you agree? Available in all sizes, downy and bronzed, they eat their yoghurts, their peaches, their sandwiches.'

Didn't any of the others ever come here, I asked.

'People who have the Aare at the bottom of their garden don't mix with the plebs.' Without being asked he added, 'I saw Claudia in town yesterday. She sends her regards, by the way.'

4

Indian Summer

Between the summer and the autumn holidays I often stayed in town during the lunch break. For lunch I took along a piece of bread and two or three apples.

On the noticeboard I compared the others' timetable with my own. It proved to be difficult to meet my new acquaintances by chance. After a week I knew that neither Bede, nor Claudia or Elizabeth were in the habit of going to the snack counter in the loggia during the long break. They also never stood outside in the porch on the side wing, nor did I ever see them walking around on the path between the main building and the playing field, although there was always a lot going on there during the breaks, lots of to-ing and fro-ing, chattering and laughter.

Should I wait for the end of the last lesson late in the afternoon? Stand near the room when Claudia's class came out? Pretend I was there quite by chance, that I was surprised to see Claudia, not pleasantly surprised, not unpleasantly surprised, simply surprised. That's how I imagined the scene. My own role was clear, but what role would the others play?

For a long time I didn't dare, and when, finally, I did and – at a safe distance – was ploughing my way through the crowds of pupils coming towards me, I only nodded to Bede as if I was in a hurry and urgently had to go on to the staircase and up to the floor above, and when I turned back and passed the room again – the door was still open – they'd all gone, only the teacher was there, busy with something at his desk.

But bumping into Claudia somewhere in town on her way to school between Römerstrasse and the Kantonsschule or on her way home between here and Römerstrasse was even more difficult. Only one thing was sure: she went home for lunch, she certainly didn't stay at school. I'd checked that by staying there myself during the lunch break every day for a week, taking several strolls through all the corridors each time. Did she cross Postplatz and Amthausplatz on her way from Römerstrasse and then pass the soldier's monument and continue along Niklausenstrasse? Or did she take the West Station underpass? Did she go through the Greiben quarter? Or through the old town? And if she did, did she cross Marktplatz or did she take the side streets?

There were far too many possibilities, and due to my own timetable there were only very few instances when I could be in the possibly right place at the right time. An accidental meeting could only be made to happen with great difficulty. After a couple of futile attempts I gave up. And I was almost relieved that a chance meeting with Claudia was so unlikely.

So I didn't go on any more strategic rides or walks, but I was still often in town, I roamed the streets whenever I could. And those bicycle rides and walks at midday and in the early evenings after school and on

Saturday afternoons usually ended in the Vorstadt, either on a bench near the vocational school directly on the Aare, or up on the Crooked Tower mound with a view down to the river and across to Postplatz. And upstream on the other bank you could see the Carrels' house.

And then one day, there she was on Wengi Bridge, coming towards me on her bicycle from the Postplatz. Elizabeth was with her. Before I realised what was happening they'd both stopped and were standing on the kerb beside me, hands resting on handlebars.

I'd have liked to have found something to ask them but I couldn't think of anything that would have led to a lengthy reply.

But it didn't matter, Elizabeth started rattling away and Claudia was there, looking my way with a serious expression on her face, and down on the Aare the north wind blew ripples across the water and the houses of the town stood there like a backdrop, and in the distance, behind and above the houses, rose the mountain.

Thinking on Monday I'd see her on Tuesday; on Wednesday trusting in tomorrow; waiting on Thursday for Friday to come; at the vegetable market on Saturday, near midday, hopes for the afternoon.

Autumn came faster than in other years. Hope six times a week makes time short, no matter how long it seems while one's waiting.

Rain, day after day. Chestnuts plumped down onto the pavement, broke out of their shells, rolled across the tarmac. This time it was Corinne who was walking beside Claudia, and again it was somewhere I hadn't expected to bump into Claudia.

Gossip about school, about films, about the theatre. 'Our Bede seems to have lost his interest in acting for good,' said Corinne. Wouldn't I like to organise something myself, now that Bede had got tired of it? To my surprise it was Claudia who asked.

We could, we ought, we should have long ago. Once again I was going to be a farmer's son in the village play, the Mixed Choir had asked me again. Having been asked I couldn't refuse, after all I had enough time.

I watched the two as they disappeared through the narrow passage by the Basel Gate.

Yes, it must have been there under the horse chestnut trees in front of the Basel Gate.The falling chestnuts bouncing over the tarmac are part of it, the chestnuts bursting out of their shells and rolling across the wet tarmac is something I remember with astonishing clarity.

And cycling home and reading Adalbert Stifter, Claudia's soporific, as Bede later teased.

Reading that book should have brought me to my senses, insofar as reading books can do any such thing. On the one hand, on the other hand. On the one hand, reading Claudia's favourite books made me emphatically aware of the disparity beween my life in the house by the stream and the Carrels' life in the villa on the banks of the Aare. More than a friendly greeting when we chanced to meet could not be expected of a girl from a family like the Carrels, could not be expected by someone like me. On the other hand – and irrationally – Stifter's female characters also taught me something else. They don't talk much, and when they do, they talk simply and about simple things. Their feelings grow slowly, which doesn't mean they grow any less strong. And after a certain point the usual consequences ensue.

The usual consequences? What did that mean for me at the time? What did I expect from Claudia after the rehearsals that summer out there in the Lee Forest glade with Bede and the whole gang?

Go back to the time when the only girls I knew closely – except for my sisters – were in books, in films and in the few plays I'd seen at the municipal theatre.

Know closely? Could I really ever get a close knowledge of girls and young women from books? All those lovely creatures in the well-bound complete works of Ganghofer or Gottfried Keller that I found in the trade union library: tender, fragile, graceful, lovable, shy, quiet, reticent, brave, delicate, courageous, modest, smiling, sensitive, compassionate. I learned everything about them, even their dreams.

But what was demonstrated there bore little relation to my own life and could hardly be applied to my own reality.

As soon as I heard that Claudia read Stifter I went and borrowed those books – *Studies*, *Colourful Stones* – from the library. What Claudia liked must be near and dear to her, and I had to read whatever was near and dear to her. I was denied the chance of hearing what she heard, of seeing what she saw; but at least I could read what she read, read what she liked. I yearned to know what she liked, to find out what moved her. I hardly dared to talk to her, but while I was reading Stifter, the distance between us disappeared; she'd been reading him for a long time and she liked reading him. Now we were reading the same thing, while reading we were absorbed in the same activity, I and she, she and I, while reading we were in the same world and anyhow by reading what she was reading I was closer to her than I could ever have been otherwise. Not that she was aware of it, but that was neither here nor there.

This world, Stifter's world, was foreign to me. It was at least as exotic as the world of Steinbeck, Faulkner, Tennessee Williams. The one was far away in the distant past, the other was in faraway America, in California, Monterey, Salinas, in Jefferson and in the cotton plantations of Louisiana.

I was astonished that Stifter and Gotthelf had written around the same time. Take Gotthelf's farmers for instance: our neighbour, farmer Furrer, was still just like them; I saw no great difference between him and Gotthelf's farmers. Mucking out, haymaking, harvesting, mowing, digging potatoes, threshing – back in nineteenth-century Emmental or in Oberdorf now, the work was much the same; even though there was now a tractor to draw the wagon, and a threshing machine standing in the barn; and there were still a couple of flails hanging on the wall in the back of the shed, as well as harnessing, as if flails and harness had just recently been used. Stifter's farmers, however, with their greenhouses and rose gardens, their furniture and pictures and their violin-playing daughters: I couldn't associate them with the couple of Oberdorf farmers

I knew. A world in which the main characters were gentlemen farmers who didn't do the ploughing, the sowing, the harvesting themselves but whose job it was to give orders and supervise the work: that world seemed to be Claudia Carrel's world.

And the women in that world, Margarita, the gentle *Obrist*'s daughter, herself gentle and good, Camilla with her moving violin playing, and Brigitta, Mathilde, Natalie: what could I learn from them? What did they tell me about Claudia? What did they demand of me? And what could I expect from a girl who, at heart, was so close to those distant creatures?

I felt that the women in Elia Kazan's films were much closer to me, even though they lived in distant America. I'd known them ever since I'd started going to the cinema. And what could they tell me, what did they exemplify? Eva Marie Saint in *On the Waterfront*, when Marlon Brando, her boyfriend, her fiancé or whatever, breaks open the door to her room so as to be near her? Vivien Leigh in *A Streetcar Named Desire*, overwrought and prim and proper, drinking whisky like water under Brando's brutally captivating stare? Carrol Baker in *Baby Doll*, on that ridiculous little iron bed, thumb in mouth, fashion magazines scattered around her on the floor? Julie Harris in *East of Eden*, the most girlish of those young women, with James Dean high up on the seat of the Ferris wheel?

Those things occurred in places that were completely different to Oberdorf, Langendorf, or the town. This town was nothing like New York, nothing like New Orleans. No Hudson here, no Salinas River, no

Mississippi, only the Aare and the streams that flowed down from the mountain into the Aare. On the Hudson and on the Mississippi, in the heat of the great city and in the heat of the south, love stories full of happiness and pain unrolled, and the young women involved in them fascinated me.

Books and films were what showed me what true life was like.

But what did true life have to do with my real life?

And what about my two sisters? Instead of learning through observation I was annoyed with them because they didn't behave like the women and girls in the films and books.

And anyway – sisters! That was a thing apart, it was something quite different, and in any case for me Katherine and Rita didn't count. I didn't see anything special in them. Nothing like Laura Wingfield, the excessively shy girl in *The Glass Menagerie*. Not a hint of the mysterious primitive passion of a Stella Kowalski in *A Streetcar Named Desire*. I could see nothing in my sisters' everyday normality that might have moved me. I couldn't or didn't want to see Katherine's anguish; her jittery behaviour, her unreliability only annoyed me.

Women couldn't help but be simultaneously cool and passionate. Or saucy, moody, superficial, corrupt – and at the same time full of hidden virtues that were only waiting to be discovered by the right man. They always had to have some hidden aim, ambivalent creatures that they were, distant, alluring, unapproachable.

5
Wasp Flight

Elizabeth's Gugelhupf cake. I see the round metal table, the coffee cups, I see the Gugelhupf and Elizabeth's head, tangles of shaggy hair down to her shoulders, I see Claudia's shoulders, her neck, I see Bede sitting beside her at the table, talking.

It must have been at the end of the autumn holidays; I'd been working on a building site again, for the Fröhlicher Company again. So it was the Saturday morning before the end of the holidays, and I was in town.

In front of the entrance to Nordmann's department store a man was demonstrating a new gadget to a group of people in a semicircle around him: saves time, saves fruit, saves vegetables, guaranteed essential to every modern home. While the man went on and on talking in his hoarse voice, his hands were busily grating cabbage and carrots, apples and pears on to a chopping board. Together with this clever grater you have this ingenious juicer, and with the juicer a brilliant potato chip and egg slicer, there you are, into the bag, you won't get these super new gadgets at this price anywhere else, who knows how many marriages they've already saved.

Non-stop performance, admission free.

Then I saw Claudia.

There she was, diagonally opposite in the semicircle of spectators, craning her slim head between the other heads. I'd been so fascinated by the one-man show that for a moment I'd forgotten my reason for being in town.

Bede was next to her, as if that was exactly as it should be.

The three of us made our way through the crowds to Amthausplatz.

'Have you ever been to any of the places here?' asked Bede. 'Come on, I'll treat you.'

Past the kiosk to the beer garden; I was taken along, it seemed quite natural.

'Shall we stay outside? There's even a bit of sunshine here now. Just what we want.'

We sat down at the metal table near the entrance.

'This town's a fog hole,' said Bede. 'How can anyone live here! The damned Aare! Another year and I bet I'll be suffering from sciatica, chronic and all over.'

I rather liked the fog, I said. Diving into the grey damp early in the morning on the way down from Oberdorf, most often already in Langendorf, or else in the avenue leading down to the town. And at midday back up into the sunshine.

'Well, well, who'd have thought it, the nature-loving village lad,' he said.

'And what about your farmhouse in the middle of the wood,' said Claudia, 'where you can play at being a hermit?'

He got up and shouted through the half-open door for the waitress.

He was on first-name terms with her, her name was Hanna.

'Hermitage my foot,' he said. 'There were workmen there all the time. They got me out of bed with their noise as early as seven. Your Adalbert Stifter would have been delighted. There's always work going on on the houses in his books. In the remotest of places, in the thickest of forests, or on the vastest, most barren of moors.'

At least house building was something I could talk about: digging foundation trenches for the house on the Heissackerweg in Langendorf.

And what had Claudia done during the holidays?

'Sat by the Aare reading Stifter,' said Bede. 'Read *Indian Summer* from beginning to end, the whole thick book, just imagine! And in between, she took driving lessons! The two things match perfectly!'

Were they quarelling? It almost seemed as if they were. But was it really a quarrel? Or were they just teasing each other? Teasing was to be expected from Bede, but Claudia surprised me. At the rehearsals in Lee Forest she'd always been reserved, taciturn, but here she was always ready with quick-witted retorts. They both knew so many things about each other, things of which I had no idea, things I'd never know.

Claudia grumbled that she had to pay for her driving lessons out of her pocket money. It was expensive and she hardly ever had the chance to practise a bit between lessons. No one wanted to give her their car, neither her father nor her mother. And they really could have, couldn't they? Especially her mother, she hardly every used her Deux Chevaux. And her sister was willing to accompany her.

'Sensible people, the Carrels,' said Bede. 'I'd never give you a car either. And I certainly wouldn't accompany you. Much too risky.'

He pulled up a chair, put his right leg up on the seat,

and the dispute about Stifter's house-building started up again.

'Anyone who reads things like that these days shouldn't even get into a car. Who in heaven's name got you on to someone like Stifter of all people? Eberhard perhaps?'

That hadn't been necessary, she said. It had been her own idea. She liked Stifter.

'A real soporific,' he said. 'All those roses and orchards, and the furniture and the pictures, i.e. all that wonderful nature stuff and all that art stuff in his page-long descriptions. Not to speak of the love stuff – it's no wonder that, a few decades later, Freud could develop his wild theories in Vienna. They form the antithesis to such a pedantically orderly world. It was all uptightness, inhibition, repression and obsessive-compulsive neurosis, nothing else.'

'You and your Freud!'

'You and your Adalbert! I just don't see how you can like someone like that. How ever could you let Eberhard talk you into reading such boring literature!'

'It's clear you've read it yourself, so it can't be that boring.'

Flies ran around on the metal table, went after the sugar cubes. There were wasps too, landing, taking off. Bede didn't let them bother him.

Now the subject was teachers.

'Eberhard! He'd do better selling graters like the man back there in front of Nordmann's. A man who likes the sound of his own voice. He's always asking us to express our opinions but never stops talking himself.'

'He's not the only one,' she said.

But Bede continued unperturbed: 'Of course, in the end the only thing that counts is what he himself thinks and says. Or take Mathys with his geography. There, for a change, you have a teacher who doesn't want to have the laziest and most stupid pupils. He wants the cleverest, the most diligent. So while we're doing tests, he simply looks out of the window across to the gym as if the Olympic Games were on there. And he only does that so that we can consult our cribs, we open them out on our desks without the slightest misgivings. He wants tables showing all the countries of South America, the varying mixtures of mestizos, mulattos, bush Indians and whites, the number per square kilometre to be given to the nearest half per cent. He himself learned it all by heart, from his exhaustive book for the most part, and now he thinks that we ought to know it too. But still, he doesn't quite believe we do, because he doesn't believe in miracles. Teachers! They're all naive.'

And while he was still in full swing we saw Elizabeth walking past on the pavement outside, couldn't be missed, what with her wild hair. We beckoned her to join us in the beer garden.

A big bag weighed down one of her shoulders. She'd got stuck with the shopping. Grumbling at the heavy work she dropped down into the chair.

'That man there,' said Bede, 'dug a trench for a house last week, so he's had experience with excavators, compressors, crowbars and goodness knows what else.'

'Okay, okay, my heavy work can't compare.' She turned to me. 'Your father's a builder, isn't he?' she asked.

'Every now and again. But he's also worked cleaning fountains for the town.'

'In that case I know him,' she said. 'I've seen a man working with a brush on the empty fountain basin out there in the square, I've seen him a couple of times. And you know, he really looks like you, honestly.'

She reached into her shopping bag and rummaged around. 'Here,' she said and placed a whitish-powdered Gugelhupf cake between the cups.

Group pantomime of watering mouths. The wasps grew more intrusive around our heads and the table.

Bede summoned Hanna. Could she give him a knife, then she could have a dusty slice too.

She went away grumpily, but soon returned with the knife and helped herself.

Cheeks filled up with soft, crumbly, pale yellow pastry. Loud munching audible all around. Elizabeth burst out laughing: 'Hanni, give me the cake knife!' She put a second slice on Bede's saucer. 'That'll shut anyone up, even a fellow like Bede.'

While I was labouring on the building site, he'd been holidaying up in Lee Forest, he said, and there he'd been among labourers too. They were repairing the roof before the winter.

Hadn't anyone visited him all the time he was there, asked Claudia.

He shook his head: 'I'm afraid not.'

'Really?'

'Not a soul. It was exquisitely pastoral and sylvan and boring.'

Claudia leaned back in her chair and said: 'What about Elizabeth?'

Looks were exchanged.

41

'I bet,' said Claudia, 'that this girl here put in an appearance.'

A frown on Bede's forehead, an exclamation mark, a question mark.

'Shall we deny it? Shall we admit it to stern Claudia?'

'There's no point denying it. We had lunch together with the roofers,' said Elizabeth.

'Cider, bread, Emmental cheese and cervelat sausage,' said Bede. 'You could have come too.'

'Was I invited?'

'Nor was she.'

Elizabeth swept crumbs from her lap, Bede acted as though he'd been caught out, Claudia nodded to them, it might have been mockingly.

And what about me, Paul Ganter, Simple Simon?

I didn't know where to look. My gaze moved sideways from Bede to Claudia, slanted past Elizabeth, concentrating on the spaces between shoulders and heads, found refuge on the remains of the Gugelhupf.

Run away with the perplexing news.

Remain seated, perplexed.

While Bede continued to pick the teachers to pieces I looked at the girl who went on uninvited visits to the Lee Forest glade. Nothing new. A wide forehead with a few pimples on the hairline, full lips and grooves from both sides of her nose down past the corners of her mouth. Tangles of shoulder-length hair.

So it was Elizabeth.

From the town to Langendorf, from Langendorf to Oberdorf the refrain, again and again: Elizabeth, not Claudia, she, not her.

It should have made me pleased. But now that I finally knew something definite, I didn't know how to go on. Things had been so much better beforehand! All I had to do was go along when taken, follow when someone went ahead, not get in anyone's way. That had come to an end now, unfortunately. The curtain went up before there'd been a rehearsal and there was no one in the prompt box.

It was all so long ago! Brought back to me now in the early morning as I sit at the kitchen table looking up to the mountain, the house still in nocturnal quiet and the first cars already driving past on Herrenweg. Some idea or other comes up, and other ideas follow, one idea after the other, it would be an exaggeration to call them thoughts, ruminations maybe, but not ruminations of the confined, gloomy kind.

Things really were odd back then!

But isn't what I'm doing now odd as well? Why did I move here into this tiny attic flat – and my wife living alone in the big house away in Winznau Marsh. What's the point? And why did I retire early although I still liked teaching, or at least I had no problem with it? Even in my last years I still enjoyed being among young people. Really? Well, yes – from time to time at least.

So many teachers give up now. Is it because everything to do with school has become difficult and troublesome? Because they're tired, because they're fed up? What is the purpose, what are their goals?

I said I wanted to finish my book on Sherwood Anderson at long last; an understandable reason, an honourable reason. But was I really serious about it? Am I still serious about it?

Why write a book on Anderson! People can live perfectly well without Anderson, even English scholars can live without Anderson, no one is waiting for another book on him. And anyway as far as I know I was the only teacher in Olten, or also here in Solothurn, who ever read any stories from *Winesburg Ohio* in class.

His characters, viewed from neither too near nor too far but seen from a kindly middle distance; their thoughts, sentiments, premonitions, their mostly very mixed feelings. The stories arise naturally out of some everyday situation; a day, or an hour, or a moment reveals what kind of person they are, a small event casts light on their entire life. Young Alice waiting for years and years for her childhood boyfriend to return from the city, having to find the courage to put up with her loneliness. The teacher Kate helping her former pupil George, now a reporter for the local paper, to break out of the confinement of the small town. Old Doctor Reefy suddenly seeing in the terminally sick hotelier's wife someone close to his heart.

Whenever I read those stories it's strange how strongly I still empathise. As though it were my own life, the same jumble of half-hearted efforts, calmly set before me by Anderson: there, look, take a good look – that's what you're like, that's what we're all like.

So why am I busying myself with my own little story instead of doing what I planned, what I told everyone I'd do, that is, write this book about Anderson and the American small town?

You think you're sensible and alert, and later it turns out that you went through all those years in a kind of daze.

'Tell me the truth, is there no one, you know what I mean, a distant acquaintance, a girlfriend, or something like that?' Anna asked on her visit yesterday evening.

'Or something like that,' I said. 'If you know someone for me, please tell me, tell me immediately please. I'd be grateful for any advice!'

Thereupon she laughed her slightly embarrassed laugh and blushed. I don't dislike seeing her laugh embarrassedly and blush during such disputes. A junior doctor who easily turns red. Perhaps she'll have to get rid of that habit.

'I only wanted to live on my own for a while, that's all.'

'That's understandable, but just don't overdo it.'

'Who's overdoing what? And anyway, it's not seemly for a father to discuss the joys and sorrows of his married life with his daughter. And as to talking about possible affairs, that would be even less seemly.'

I don't mind being alone early in the morning. I look forward to sitting alone at the kitchen table, listening to the news, drinking coffee. No, I don't mind being alone.

In the evening it's different sometimes. Sometimes, by no means always.

III

THE GANTERS BY THE STREAM – VILLAGE THEATRICALS

'I am not a leader of men, Willy, and neither are you. You were never anything but a hard-working drummer who landed in the ash can like all the rest of them!'

Arthur Miller, *Death of a Salesman*

1
Potato Economy

The second month of that summer of fifty-nine – I'm sure I can reconstruct what it was like, at least roughly. I remembered it often enough later on: the walks to Hazel Wood, the walks along the wheatfields in the morning, in the afternoon, again late in the evening, all tensed up, saddled with the crazy plan to write three plays.

The summer of the previous year too, the summer before that summer; starting with the rehearsals in the Lee Forest glade, then the secret visits to the house on the Aare, the walks through the town, always in the hope of bumping into Claudia; then in late autumn and in winter the visits to the cinema, the pubs, the jealousy, all the strange premieres and their sequels, that awful spring: I can probably summon all that up again, more or less, although it's all so far away, and however much I might have forgotten.

But what about the time before, before that business with Claudia? How things were before and how they still were in the midst of that Claudia business, suddenly perceived by me as I'd never perceived them before, things that couldn't be brushed aside because they were a part of me like it or not, all those Ganter stories and Ganter past histories: will I be able to recall all that too?

Racks piled with potatoes – in the cellar, near the stream, damp and cool, the potatoes kept until the spring. For breakfast at six, almost always at midday, and in the evening anyway. As fried potatoes, potato soup, mashed potatoes, potatoes sliced or cut into sticks, halved and quartered, boiled, served with braised onions, scattered with breadcrumbs, with chives, with parsley, in a white sauce. Cheese potatoes, potatoes with dried pears or dried apple slices, potatoes in their jackets, with blueberry sauce, blackberry compote, apple purée. And nearly always double recipes, as they were nearly always also heated up again to give breaded mashed potato patties with egg, boiled potatoes with pasta, or soup from leftovers.

In October the racks were full, around Christmas the piles were visibly smaller, in March the wooden boards appeared underneath, by mid-May we had to get new supplies from the Furrers' big cellar. At a special price: in exchange we helped the Furrers with their potato harvest every autumn, even Karin couldn't get out of it.

As long as our grandmother was alive things went reasonably well. She did the housework and also gave the Furrers a hand. Mother worked for Roamer Watch. Like many of the Oberdorf women who were only semi-skilled she didn't earn much at the watch factory, but it was a regular income.

It was an essential part of our household budget. Father often changed his job, he could seldom stick it out in the same place for more than a year. Mostly it was he who gave in his notice, or else he simply walked off one day. Arguments with his boss about work assignments, expenses, overtime, and suddenly his stowed up anger would break out. 'Screw you! You can go to hell.' Which didn't stop him taking on a job with the same company the following year. He must have worked for the builders Fröhlicher & Co at least half a dozen times over the years.

On top of that, the misery of payday. He might have come home punctually for supper every day for a fortnight – but once he felt those three or four fifty-franc notes in his breastpocket on a Friday evening, arriving home punctually became difficult. Payday had to be celebrated, that was the custom among the builders, and Ganter would have been the last not to join in. As he went into the pub with his mates he resolved to drink only one bottle, or two at the most. But the fun often went on until closing time, sometimes continued on Saturday or Sunday mornings, frequently came up again on Monday evening. Not till then could peace return for the next fortnight.

Fortnightly beer theatricals. Not something Mother put up with in silence, needless to say. On payday Fridays, at breakfast already, she'd start appealing to Father's conscience. He was to come home straight after work this time. We desperately needed the money. The rent hadn't been paid yet, not to mention the health insurance and last year's taxes. He could go and have a pint after supper, no one would mind that.

Her remonstrances were usually in vain. And then, when he finally showed up at midnight he was met with a litany of reproaches. What was said on such occasions had been known for years. As a rule it was that he was a man without a trace of character, a wet rag who let himself be kept away from his most basic duties by his wonderful friends, who ran after everyone like a three-year-old child, a good for nothing who thought only of slaking his thirst and who forgot his wife and children at the first drop of beer. If we were particularly short of money at the time he was called a scoundrel, a ruffian, a drunk, from the start, and because that didn't have the required effect she confronted him with all the old stories bit by bit, too much was too much, she couldn't stand it any longer, hadn't been able to for a long time, and if he went on like that she'd leave him or have him put under guardianship.

Father knew perfectly well what to expect under the circumstances, and it might sometimes have been precisely for fear of meeting with a particularly unholy row that he kept away from home once suppertime and the grace period had gone by. On the way home he had to prepare himself. If he believed things didn't look too bad he invented an excuse: even with the best of intentions, he hadn't been able to do anything else as he'd bumped into various people, had been taken along here and there, one thing had followed from the other, the way it is, and suddenly, he didn't know how, it had got late, which was something that could happen to anyone once in a while. However, if he feared that the big guns would be brought out he talked himself into a mighty fury in advance, and was on the ready with all kinds of accusations on his part so as to be able to fight back. Crossing the Furrers' forecourt, the rehearsal; passing the manure heap, the big soliloquy

– what need of footlights, at no other time is life so clearly behind and below him. Even if the play is a mess, he does his best acting, stamping naturalistically up the stairs after midnight, coughing as he comes into the kitchen, cursing along the back corridor and past the living room, here I am, Paul Ganter, it was good fun and that's all that matters.

And then the final scene, scolding back and forth, a far from happy end. Above the double bed there's a picture in a gilded frame, a genuine oil painting: a woman with thick blonde pinned-up hair reclining on a sheepskin in a pink nightdress, to her right and left some wisps of cloud and on either side a little angel with bobbed hair, silent witnesses to the late homecoming, the same old song and dance time after time.

Stinginess was the last thing my father could have been accused of. But his frequent job changes and his disastrous payday habit resulted in the need for constant penny-pinching.

And that's exactly what he hated most. If he was treated to a glass of beer he reciprocated by buying a round, even if it meant putting it on the slate; he always had some small debt in at least one of the pubs in the area. When it had piled up, he steered well clear of that pub until the next payday. But then, because he had to show how creditworthy he was, he'd stay there all evening carousing with two or three companions. No big sums were involved, only a couple of rounds of beer. If I'd done the same later on with my salary as a teacher, I'd hardly have felt it. In his case, however, just one bout of generosity was enough to disrupt our finances for weeks.

And the measures he took to redress the financial situation easily turned into the opposite. For example, he took on small building jobs: after hours, or on Saturday afternoons, he cemented washhouse floors, drives, garden walls; and then, having sweated for a few extra hours, he felt it was only right that he should get something out of it for himself too, and had a hearty drink before going home.

In pubs, in particular, there was always something that needed extending or converting. There's hardly a pub in Oberdorf, Langendorf or Rüttenen where there isn't some small wall that was built by Ganter for cash in hand. For when his debts had piled up – thanks to his generosity in standing everyone drinks – he was magnanimously given a chance to work them off. There wasn't much in it for him, at the most it paid off his debts. Often he made new ones while settling the old ones.

Bleak things come to mind. And instead of doing what I intended, I dig around in those old stories. As if I hadn't given them enough thought already.

But have I really? Have I really pondered over the whole affair? True, now and then something on the subject ran through my head, by some coincidence I was reminded of one thing or another. But did I really give it much thought? And anyway, is there any sense in thinking about it?

2
'Move, you must keep moving ...'

Move, you must keep moving, or you won't get anywhere! It was a motto that had already been a guideline for his father, my grandfather, then still the proud owner of a small building business. They say he hardly ever managed to stand being on a building site for more than an hour at a time.

He'd stroll through the village with architectural plans under his arm, he'd make excursions to neighbouring villages and down to town, still on a bicycle of course and not for pleasure. Business matters were generally dealt with at a pub table, where it was cool in summer and pleasantly warm in winter. His head remained fully operational with wine, not sour wine of course, he owed himself that, what with his flourishing business, the four labourers he employed. Bragging was Ganter's strong point, he wasn't too particular about arithmetic. He looked ahead with confidence, the future was rosy, people would always need houses, soon he'd have to employ another bricklayer and several more labourers. In that fuddled state he let himself be talked into providing a couple of loan guarantees. A man like Ganter, he thought, can surely afford that, can't he?

But he couldn't, he went bankrupt.

And suddenly that was that: no more walking around with plans under his arm, no more offers and invoices in the pig leather briefcase, no more management from the pub table. The house on the village square and the shed in Lee Lane came under the hammer. From under his nose his close acquaintances and best friends carried off tools, machines, scaffolding, all the paraphernalia for a pittance.

Gloating over other people's misfortune is a most honourable pleasure and it should not be begrudged his friends in the village. Yet in retrospect it became apparent that, by virtue of his mobile life style, Ganter had been a few steps ahead of them, a harbinger of the Great Depression: soon others would be in for it too.

My father had just turned eighteen. His mother, my grandmother, now went out to work in the factory. The business and the house were gone. We were in rented accommodation, just scraping by. Ganter the builder couldn't stand it in the village any longer, he retreated to the Oberaargau and then to Central Switzerland. But his wife soon got used to the new life, kept herself to herself, went punctually to the Roamer Watch factory on weekdays, rushed to church on Sundays.

Her husband never showed up. Only much later when his health was failing did he remember that he had a wife to whom he was married and whom he'd left behind as a factory worker in Oberdorf. Whenever he failed to find a job for a few weeks he'd turn up out of the blue and ask for board and lodging.

The boy, my father, had also left. He'd just turned eighteen when he had to go and eat foreign bread. It was an expression he used later too. 'Eating foreign bread,' he'd say, 'is good for everyone, it never did anyone any harm.' His apprenticeship in his father's building business had been cut short, now he was learning the geography of Switzerland. He worked in Reinach, in Muttenz, near Liestal for a while, then in Möhlin on the Rhine, and also in Baar, in Menzingen, and ended up for a year in Gossau in Canton St Gallen. At the age of seventeen he'd worked as the foreman and site manager whenever his old man was on a pub crawl on business; now he was employed as a labourer even though he did the work of a bricklayer. That's what his career was like. He lived in rented rooms, sometimes sharing a room with two or three others. From time to time, seldom rather than often – for example at Christmas, Easter or Whitsun, or on Assumption Day for the annual village fair – he came back to the village and visited his mother.

His years away from home would come in useful later on, in the present they were disagreeable, as a thing of the past they provided him with stories to recount. He'd got around a lot, more anyway than most of the Oberdorf fellows of his age, who'd only seen a bit of Switzerland while they were in military training.

For him there was no military training; although he specially came to Solothurn on the call-up day, he was discharged, ostensibly because there was something wrong with his back. In Eastern Switzerland, in Central Switzerland, in Baselland he went from one building site to the next, a smart alec, a jack of all trades, a real whizz-kid; he lived for the moment and wherever there was fun he'd be there with his big mouth.

In Schönenwerd he met my mother.

She was the second of three sisters. She worked in the Bally shoe factory, punching holes in leather pieces or gluing shoe soles, piecework. That was on weekdays.

A postcard-size photograph shows her sitting stiffly on a garden bench in her Sunday dress, with a straw hat on her curly hair, her hands in her lap. My father is standing behind the chair, his cap pulled over his forehead, a cigarette hanging crookedly from the corner of his mouth.

Father's Claudia story? Perhaps.

It was a time of economic crisis. People had to be glad not to lose their jobs overnight. From time to time there was a road to be widened or a piece of Aare marshland to be drained, but otherwise there wasn't much building work around. Not till after 1937 did things improve. That's when they got married.

Young Ganter's return to the village on the mountain slope above the town. Follow the Wildbach upstream, the road shaded by ash trees. No need for a removals van, they were nobodies, they had nothing. Across the main forecourt of the Furrers' house, past the manure heap, past the garden: Here we are again. The new family was launched.

That's what the mother, now also mother-in-law, then grandmother, had long been waiting for. Her wish had been fulfilled, you shouldn't always be pessimistic. She stopped going to the factory, the young woman took her place – anyone who has punched holes in leather or glued shoe soles can drill holes in watch components, or polish watchcases. There was someone there to do the cooking, the cleaning, the washing, to mend clothes to attend to the kitchen garden. And there was someone there to bring in some extra earnings, not much, but something at least. The roles were allotted, the household functioned reasonably well.

But before long the two women clashed. Oberdorf is known for its harsh climate. What exactly did they quarrel about? Everything and nothing. My father preferred to turn a blind eye, he'd tried to mediate, but without success. It was difficult for him to act as a referee when increasingly he himself was the cause of the dispute. Both women wanted to reform him and each blamed the other for his escapades.

Then the war broke out. The border occupation eased the pressure on the home front, the running battle was fought between the two women alone now that father had been called up. As a reserve soldier he built bunkers, first in the area around Basel, then in the Bernese Oberland. He often hit his fingers, which put him out of action for days on end.

Away from home he livened up. Here he knew how to defend himself, he still had his ready tongue. In Interlaken he was in hospital for a long time with serious blood poisoning. 'Rub zis man wiz iodine,' said the doctor, a French-speaking Swiss, on his daily visits. The blood poisoning led to iodine poisoning, but Ganter's morale didn't suffer. The photo album in the sideboard drawer later contained several postcards, all of them with the lake and snowy mountains in the background. After a good recovery, the reservist was allowed to go home for a spell.

Shortly before the outbreak of the war Katherine had been born, I followed two years later. Rita, the baby, came nine months after demobilisation.

The old routines were taken up again. Children were just one of those things, they didn't make things easier. Grandmother forbade almost everything and let us do more or less as we pleased. When Mother came home in the evening she was met with long-winded complaints about us. We knew we wouldn't have to suffer any consequences. In any case, said Mother, it was Grandmother's own fault. Scolding alone was no use. She'd brought the children's father up in the same stupid way and you could see the result. Father only seldom intervened. He'd thrash our bottoms with the carpet-beater, he warned. But it never went beyond threats, we were never beaten.

On the other hand, he was well-known in the village for his fits of rage. There were children in the neighbourhood who ran away as soon as they saw him, even from afar, coming down Weissensteinstrasse. If something hadn't worked, if something had got in his way, he'd start swearing, cursing, slinging his tools all over the place. Then he'd leave everything just where it was and not come home until long after we'd gone to bed. We were awoken when the front door slammed and he tramped up the stairs, threw his nailed shoes onto the tiled floor, and we heard Mother go out into the kitchen.

As a child you have no choice who to like and who not to like. You take what's on offer. You wouldn't even want to swap.

3

Union Representative

In for a penny, in for a pound. Now that Grandfather had let the business go to ruin, my father could at least be something completely different. Propelled by the economic crisis and his travels, he moved left from the capsized middle classes and, once he was back in Oberdorf, that's where he stayed. Paul Ganter could use his head and he could use his tongue, long live the union, long live class warfare!

For a while he was a dues collector for the Union of Construction and Timber Workers. When he visited the union members and brought them their contribution stamps, he often took one of us children with him. In that way we got to know the labourers, the plasterers, the painters, the bricklayers, the Italians of Oberdorf. Builders are immediately recognisable by their hands, even after work. I was allowed to stick the contribution stamps into the booklets while their heavy fingers counted the money out on the table. Many were permanently in arrears. 'Next week things will be better, Paul,' they said. 'Come again next Saturday.' In every house a different smell. I saw kitchens and living rooms, the women fed me sweets or biscuits. Here my father was an important man, he was treated with respect, he was offered a chair, asked to sit down for a moment.

To my mother, however, this function brought more trouble than renown. As a union representative my father always had an extra excuse to go to the village, and if he didn't take along Katherine, Rita or me he nearly always got stuck in some pub or other: the Rössli, the Kreuz, the Sternen, the Engel, the Helvetia. He'd grown up here, everyone knew him, and in the two hours he spent running up and down the village collecting dues, he'd be sure to bump into someone who was thirsty and wanted to go for a drink. Of course he couldn't refuse the invitation. The only trouble was that on those village rounds he had other people's money in his pocket besides his own, so that when, in the course of those friendly carousings, he'd run out of the latter, he was tempted to pay for the following halves and pints with the former. However, in my father's view, embezzling union funds would have been such a capital sin that it was absolutely out of the question. So my mother always made up the deficit with the housekeeping money.

Once the difficult accounting had been done and the exact sum handed over down to the last cent, there'd be a long period when Father came home punctually every evening, rolled his cigarettes himself, drank mint tea before going to bed, suggested of his own accord that we bring him his midday meal over to the building site. However, the more he stinted himself, the surer he was to kick over the traces after a few weeks, to live it up on payday Fridays, to fulminate in the pubs against slave-drivers, good-for-nothing factory bosses, the Free Democrats gang, demand the abolition of struggle and toil, call his comrades wet rags, lame ducks, call for men to fight as men used to fight, proclaim a general strike.

At a time when the good Swiss were benefiting from the Cold War, the rumour went round that Ganter was not a real socialist, that he was a communist. Mother was sacked by Roamer Watch, later on by Lanco too. He himself changed jobs even more frequently than before. Nothing could have stopped him making all the better use of his gift of the gab.

He never went to church, he railed against the coal bags, as he called the clergy, made fun of incense and all the mumbo-jumbo, and every Sunday he sported a tie as red as the ribbon he wore on his lapel on Labour Day. On Labour Day he didn't work in the kitchen garden like the other Oberdorf people, he didn't build a little wall on the side, he didn't climb the Weissenstein or the Balmfluhkopf in search of the spring. Down in the town he joined the parade with the weatherbeaten faces, the lame, the misshapen, the gout-ridden, he stood near the front of the thin gathering listening to the speech, arise you wretched of the earth, the day would be duly celebrated with drinks, the second of May would be a holiday too.

After Mother had lost her job a second, then a third time she refused to go back to the factory. It was his fault, she said. His stupid talk in the pubs had got her put on the black list.

She would only have been able to work part-time anyway. Grandmother had died and Rita couldn't always be given to the Furrers to look after when Katherine and I were at school.

4
'High Noon at Midnight'

This is what it looks like in the trilogy:

On the left to the rear of the stage, a table with five stools. The father and the mother in the kitchen around midnight. And in the left front, near the apron, the director; he introduces the scene while the son, the young hero, sits in the right front dangling his legs over the edge of the stage.

LISA SCHLATTER: Well?

WILLY SCHLATTER: What do you mean, well?

LISA SCHLATTER: Where's your pay?

WILLY SCHLATTER: My pay packet. My pay packet, that's the only thing you're interested in! Here you are, here's your money, here you can have it all. *(With a vigorous movement he throws her a small yellow envelope across the table.)* Go on, count it!

LISA SCHLATTER: *(At first she leaves the envelope on the table, but then picks it up after all, opens it, pulls out three banknotes.)* Is that all?

WILLY SCHLATTER: Isn't that enough for you? Your own fault, other women manage with less.

LISA SCHLATTER: I'd like to see them, you must show them to me some time. All right, what happened? You can't have drunk up all of fifty francs in one evening. Did you have debts you had to pay back?

WILLY SCHLATTER: Fifty piddling francs, you'll get them next week, don't worry. No one will starve before then, will they?

LISA SCHLATTER: And where in heaven's name are you going to find fifty francs next week if you haven't got them now, today, on your payday?

WILLY SCHLATTER: Geiser still owes me a sum, he'll give it to me on Monday, at the latest on Tuesday, he promised me, without fail, word of honour.

LISA SCHLATTER: You and Geiser, without fail and word of honour! You think you're so clever but, as far as money's concerned, anyone, no matter how dim he is, can wrap you round their little finger. He offers you a drink, promises you something or other, promises pie in the sky, and you believe him, and in the end you pay for the beer yourself although he'd invited you. But it never occurs to you that Stella and Laura have been waiting for new shoes since last winter and that you yourself need a new jacket, no you never think of that, you don't waste a minute thinking of it. Your mate Geiser is more important to you, you've been hoping and waiting all week to spend an evening boozing around with a fellow like Geiser. You think you're so clever, you think you're the smartest person in the world. And then you get taken in by the first crook to come your way. It's always the same with you.

WILLY SCHLATTER: Oh yes, as long as you have something to grumble about! You've been waiting all day to pour out your tales of woe. But no, what am I saying – you've been waiting all week, that's the only thing you've had in mind all week: longing for it to be Friday at last and for me to come home late. And it's not my pay packet you're waiting for, it isn't money that you want. It's the chance to bleat, nothing else, all you're waiting for is an excuse to have a good moan. If I'd come to supper on time, you'd be feeling something was missing and that the week hadn't ended as it should. Be honest, admit it, admit it just this once, you know, I know, and you know that I know: All you want is a fight. You're just waiting for a chance to do some scolding. Otherwise life's too boring for you. You're not capable of coming quietly into the kitchen here and heating up my food, the scraps that've been left over, oh no, you can't do that, that would be too much to expect, it wouldn't satisfy you, it'd be too boring. And if I came at nine, and even if I came as early as eight or even seven, I bet it would be exactly the same, not the slightest difference. So it doesn't depend on when I come, how I come or if I come at all. So I might as well stay at the Frohsinn as long as it suits me, as long as I'm having fun. For no matter what time I come home, early or late, there's sure to be someone waiting here to stuff up my ears with her bellyaching. Bellyaching and complaining, that's what you're good at, you're a champion, you can beat anyone. But it's never occurred to you that things could be different. In other words that I might simply come home on a Friday – early or late, it doesn't make any difference – that I'd simply come home and sit down here in the kitchen, that I'd come home nice and quietly and that someone would heat up my food and I'd sit at the table and nothing else, just sit at the table, and eat something, that's all. For I haven't eaten anything yet tonight, I didn't have time to eat, I had other things to do. But you won't understand that, it's something you'll never understand, it's too complicated for you. You sit in your kitchen, sit there surrounded by your bits and bobs, pondering all Friday long what you want to whine about, what accusations you want to make. If only there was something new about your whingeings, but no, you're like a broken record, I know what you're going to say, I know it by heart, I don't even listen any more, there's no point in listening, as far as I'm concerned you can curse and swear until you're blue in the face, I don't listen any more, I can't put up with it any more, blah blah blah …

(*He speaks more and more quietly, his voice sounds like in a radio play as the voice gradually gets faded out. At the same time the light on the back part of the stage gets dimmer and goes out.*)

THE DIRECTOR (*in the spotlight front left*): That's how it always was and so it continues. And the young man over there (*the Director points across to the other side of the apron stage*), the involuntary listener and spectator, slips into the role of a reporter and describes it all as a war, trench warfare, as a battle fought again and again but never lost or won.

BRUNO: The long time of waiting is over. Forward march, to the midnight battle. Guns at the ready, attack is the best defence. Is it the great, the decisive battle? It's only the running battle at the kitchen table. Ordinary ammunition is used, there's enough available, supplies are plentiful, good-for-nothing and bastard and boozer, silly cow, stupid cow, lazy cow. Duds, non-starters, a racket, much ado about nothing. It lasts for a while, then it's over, and in two weeks it'll start up again. Forward forward into war, let's fight until our throats are sore, never give up the fight, victory beckons tonight.

It's a bit embarrassing, I must say, to have that kind of thing in the original before one's eyes after more than forty years, typewritten, the print faded, the paper yellowed. A table, a stool, a nagging woman. On the other side, a blustering man making spiteful comments. It was something I might have remembered at any time. However, the hero commenting on the squabble in the pose of a war reporter, that was a detail I'd completely forgotten.

Claudia was to see how closely I'd been affected by it all – and how far, and how stolidly, I now stood above it all. I probably wanted her to see both how ugly those performances were and how I managed to make fun of it all. At the same time I was probably thinking of Bede: someone like Bede, had he been in my situation, would doubtless have made fun of it.

In the trilogy the pubs are named Eintracht, Harmonie, Frohsinn: that too was meant to be scornfully ironic. It was to be a decidedly modern play. Pictures would be projected on to the stage wall with a slide projector, brownish old photographs: a house with a shed, clearly recognisable as a building company – a man in a soldier's uniform, a sapper in the Second World War – bombed houses in Schaffhausen – road-building – and of course the inn signs Frohsinn, Eintracht, Harmonie.

Oberdorf became Hubel, Langendorf Fallern, and I named the town Schleipfen. The hero's family received the gloomy sounding name Schlatter. With Claudia's family I hesitated a long time between Tacier and Rossier, but it seemed to have escaped my notice that whichever I chose it was a clear hint at the French name of Carrel. Claudia became Margarita, her best friend Elizabeth became Clarissa, and I gave Bede the alias Thomas.

I had already thought up a lot of this on my excursion to Zurich, after the cold night in the allotments on the margins of the wood above Hadlaubsteig. I remember sitting on a bench on Lindenhofplatz the morning after and writing down the names in the stiff-covered exercise book. Trying to find new names like that was a pleasure. Later on, when it came to inventing dialogues between these newly named people, my pleasure and enthusiasm soon declined. However, now that I'd started writing a trilogy I had to finish it – and without dialogues it couldn't be done.

'Erica, it was Erica above all who wanted children.'
'And you didn't?'
'No, I wasn't particularly keen.'
'So I'm actually an unwanted daughter.'
'Is that how you feel?'

'Not really. It's a question I've never asked myself.'

'In that case, I've been lucky again. A family with children and all, something I'd never had much faith in, something I don't have the fondest memories of myself. Or rather, I have rather mixed memories and I'd probably have managed quite well staying single all my life.'

'As can be seen right now!'

'Admittedly, particularly now. A kind of bachelor again, without family life, away from wife and children. But you aren't children any more, not by a long way. By the way, was it bad, I mean, did I really perform so poorly as a father?'

'Poorly? Of course not. In fact the way you sometimes took care of our little worries was quite exemplary. No, really, you can't be said to have shirked your paternal duties.'

'That's nice to hear – specially from you!'

'Why specially from me?'

'You were quite a difficult child at times. Sometimes you annoyed me five times in one day, at least five times. Have you forgotten how cheeky and how rebellious your behaviour was?'

'That's something that must have escaped me. I don't know anything about it. Cheeky, rebellious? All right, George perhaps, but not me! And even if so, we were only defending ourselves against Erica, and that was necessary. Admit it, it was imperative. It's not that easy to grow up in a household where people are always talking about school, school for breakfast, school for dinner, school for supper. It gets to be too much after a while, especially if, like George just before his finals, you more or less hate school. And Erica is the one who decides – you know how, without ever raising her voice – she decides everything exactly as she's worked it out in her head. She always knows what's right, what's most sensible, what's best. That can really get on your nerves. Admit it, it gets on your nerves after a while.'

'You're being catty!'

'Catty? I'm only giving a diagnosis.'

Woke up even earlier than usual today, at half past four. Even with all three windows open all night the thermometer still shows a temperature of over twenty degrees, and this heatwave has already lasted three whole weeks. There hasn't even been a thunderstorm to cool the air.

What was the summer like the year the Claudia story began with those rehearsals in Lee Forest? And what about the summer the following year, the summer I wrote that awful trilogy? There'll have been hot days and weeks, but I can't remember anything like this heatwave. No, as to the weather, they were probably average summers, it's not the weather that makes me remember that summer and the summer before.

Soft birdsong from afar, chattering magpies close by. A car starts up, drives away. And again the birdcalls 'Coocoocoo … coocoocoo', soft, prolonged, from far away: pigeons, wood pigeons perhaps. When I was still a primary school teacher I'd have been sure to have had the right answer ready.

Claudia's father had recorded the diffuse chirruping on his Revox recorder. There are just as many bushes and trees in the gardens around here as there were down there on the banks of the Aare. Carrel the sound hunter, birdsong, house concerts.

And the luxury now of being able to think about those old things. Social advancement – what a joke! On the one hand yes, and nevertheless no. Simply sitting on a wooden stool at the kitchen table, did I really ever want anything else?

5

'Why ever didn't I become a bricklayer!'

At the rehearsals in Lee Forest I'd already found out that Claudia's father was an engineer for Autophon. The house by the stream and the house on the Aare, and then Autophon: surely it was more than just a coincidence.

After I'd started at the teacher training college I used to pass that factory several times a day. It meant something special to me, since I also knew it from the inside: before going to the training college I'd started a commercial apprenticeship there. Not that I remembered any engineer of the name of Carrel, although I'd probably run into him at the time when, as an apprentice in the internal post department, I went to his department to place letters and documents in the in-tray and to pick up the documents from the out-tray for further distribution.

My start at Autophon – and the speedy end.

I remember the big room in which the exam was held. Most of the other young people were here for apprenticeships as electrical mechanics, I was here for a commercial apprenticeship.

Late one afternoon two or three weeks after that, my father and I were in the office of the personnel manager to sign the apprenticeship contract. Father had come home in the middle of the afternoon and had put on his Sunday clothes, he'd even put on a tie. 'The things we do for those pencil pushers. And now you want to be a pencil pusher like them. Oh well.' We'd taken the bus to town.

We went back on foot. I remember us walking together through the driving snow to the crossing down by the post office, going up Weissensteinstrasse and through Langendorf, trudging home along the stream through the falling dusk. The snow fell in large flakes and the damp got into my shoes. Like my father I'd put on my Sunday clothes, the beige herringbone trousers and jacket, the same suit I wore a year later for the teacher's college entrance exam.

But for the moment I was looking forward to starting at Autophon the following spring. During my third year at secondary school I'd given the choice of a career careful thought. Both of my teachers had been astonished that I hadn't wanted to register for the teacher's college entrance exam. But another four years of school, and without any earnings all that time, was too much to ask of my family. Not that I'd ever discussed it with anyone, it was something I'd decided by myself. A commercial apprenticeship only lasted three years, and

I'd be earning apprentice wages. Later on I could still become a teacher, of commercial subjects, shorthand for example, that's what I'd read in the careers book.

As soon as I'd secured the job at Autophon I started to prepare for it systematically in the time that was left. In December I'd completed a correspondence course for English, so now I'd be able to use English in my budding career as an office clerk. In addition I'd teach myself shorthand up to the spring. And if I'd had the money I'd have bought a Hermes typewriter so as to learn touch typing before starting on the job. I looked forward confidently to the start of my apprenticeship.

The first two weeks I worked in the storeroom, then in the internal mail department. There was a strict plan according to which I'd get to know all the departments and their work. Everything went well, the storeman who instructed me, the young woman in the mail department, the other people too, they were all kindly and ready to help.

Nevertheless, after a couple of days the initial feeling of joyful suspense was gone, replaced by a sense of unease I was almost ashamed of. The things I had to do made sense, and yet I couldn't work up any enthusiasm. No matter how attentive and willing I was, the desks, the trays and the filing cabinets, the accounting machines, all the secretarial work and the people there, the way they talked, the way they behaved – everything continued to be remote and unfamiliar. It had nothing to do with Autophon, I knew – in any other firm it would have been exactly the same.

I can see myself in the midday break, sitting behind the factory building, I can see myself walking through the town, full of doubts, increasingly uneasy. Yet I'd given my future career such careful thought! Once more I listed all the reasons in support of holding on to the decision I'd made the previous winter. The work at Autophon was easy, I had no trouble with commercial subjects, and I'd always have plenty of time to devote to things that had nothing to do with office life. I could continue to learn English on the side, I could start learning Italian, could learn Spanish, could go in for amateur theatricals, go to the cinema, I could read all the books in the Typographia Union library. Something I'd so carefully planned and maturely pondered for months: Could I truly believe that my decision had been wrong and mistaken after only a few days experience? Surely I couldn't.

And yet, that's exactly what I had to admit, I had no choice. Office work was nothing for me. Better become a bricklayer, or a carpenter, or a tiler. The decision to do a commercial apprenticeship had been wrong.

All the more so because another decision was ripe, had indeed been ripe for a long time: the decision to take the entrance exam to the teacher's college. I'd missed it for this year, so now I had to wait till next spring. Although that meant an unwelcome loss of time, it also involved a gain; for if I broke off my apprenticeship immediately I could find a job with a building company and earn almost a whole year's pay, I could earn a lot more than I'd have earned in all my three years as an apprentice. Why hadn't it occurred to me sooner? In all my deliberations about my choice of career I'd never made the calculation. So simple!

My father had never objected to my commercial apprenticeship, and he didn't mind my breaking it off now either. 'One pencil pusher less, great!'

Only my mother had her doubts. 'Changing jobs, that's something the Ganters are good at,' she said. 'And we all know what that leads to. And what if you fail the entrance exam?' She had to take charge of everything, and now she saw new worries coming her way.

Shortly afterwards, when I received my first wage, she took it for granted that I'd hand it over, the whole sum. My idea had been that I'd only give her what I'd have earned if I'd stayed on in my apprenticeship. I would have put the rest in the bank in reserve for my four years at college when I wouldn't be able to earn anything. It seemed so sensible that I'd never discussed it with my mother. But when I brought home my first pay packet the household budget happened to be in a critical state, as so often.

Without protest I handed over the money. But then I ran out of the kitchen and down the stairs, ran along Haselweg towards the woods, fighting my rising tears. I was about to venture something new and all my mother thought of was unpaid bills.

It was quite true, nearly everything my father did was wrong, and yet I was somehow fond of him. On the other hand, everything my mother did was always right, yet I never really managed to give her credit for it.

She'd kept the exercise books with their stiff covers, the ring binders containing the trilogy, the file with the drafts. Last autumn as we were clearing out her flat in Zurich Erica found the cardboard box in the wall cupboard. I hadn't known that my mother had taken those old things with her to Zurich, she'd never said anything about it to me.

We seldom saw each other, and if it hadn't been for Erica and the children, we'd probably have visited her even less often. After my father died she moved to Zurich, through one of her cousins she found a two-room flat in Plattenstrasse, less than ten minutes on foot from the university. Anna went to her place for a meal almost once a week when she first started at the university. And George even lived with her for a semester.

Why had she taken the old rubbish with her when she moved from Oberdorf to Zurich? Why that rubbish and not some other rubbish? Why my school things and not those of my two sisters too? And had she ever even opened the box to see what was inside? No, she wasn't likely to have read anything in the exercise books.

'But in Winznau you were always active, weren't you?'

'On the school board, little jobs like that? What of it! I was asked and I couldn't very well say no. I had to deal with that kind of thing every day as it was.'

'What about the Socialists? Weren't you a member of the party executive for a while?'

'I wrote the minutes, yes. Managing the accounts and writing the minutes, those are two things no one's keen to take on, they're glad if someone else does it. And as I don't like bookkeeping I did the minutes, I did that for a couple of years.'

'I don't do anything at all, all I do is pay my subscription to Amnesty.'

'At least you do that. And didn't you go to the demonstration in Bern last spring?'

'The Iraq nonsense? It so happened I had the day off. A friend phoned, she didn't want to go alone, would I go with her. I also asked Benno, but he only laughed. It was no use demonstrating in Bern against people like Bush, Blair or Berlusconi, he said.'

'And unfortunately Benno was right.'

'Nevertheless, I don't regret having gone. It's something I took over from you two, by the way, you took us with you a couple of times.'

'You don't mean the May First parades in Olten, do you? Not exactly mass demonstrations, never were.'

'Big or small, real outings or only in Olten, I always enjoyed them anyway. And then there was that enormous one, Kaiseraugst or something.'

'Can you remember that? Of course we were there, although only after it was nearly over. We also prevented them from building the Graben nuclear power station. The things we prevented after we'd let them set up the cooling tower in Gösgen right in front of our noses! By the way, taking you to those demonstrations and making a full-scale family excursion out of it was Erica's idea, and she had a clever explanation for it.'

'Really?'

'From an early age you and George used to watch us fill in the ballot forms and of course you used to ask what it was all about. More often than not you also came with us to the polling station at the school.'

'Yeah, I remember, a kind of ritual – I was allowed to throw Erica's envelope into the ballot box and George did the same with your envelope.'

'Afterwards of course you wanted to know the results. Did the other people in Winznau vote the same as your parents? Naturally, most often they didn't. And that's why Erica thought we had to show you at least once that people who lose at the elections and referendums might be a minority, but that it is often a large minority. Look around you, we're not alone, all those people who're marching together are fighting for the same thing. We may often lose, but we're still many more than just a few. Clearly it was a demonstration that functioned, and you still have a tendency to manifest publicly that you are for something or against it. There you see how far-sighted and clever your mother is.'

'Oh stop it, of course you're right. And Erica is always right anyhow.'

Woke up at five. The mist between the houses surprised me.

Down the stairs and out of the house, along Herrenweg, towards the sun. In front of me above the border of trees, the bright orange-tinted sky. The street lamps are still on, pinpoints of light reflected in the long window façade of the Kantonsschule. The lamps lighting up the dawn seem strangely superfluous, like stage lighting they've forgotten to switch off. No lights in the houses. Holiday time, only a moped and two or three cars come towards me. Probably people on their way to work.

Then, global politics in the kitchen: a dispute between the British government and the BBC. The government, with the help of Murdoch's private stations, is trying to throw doubts on the BBC's accuracy. It's still the Kelly affair: alleged weapons of mass destruction in Iraq, the dossier had been manipulated, said Kelly, and now he's dead. But my comrade Blair is sure to manage to get the matter straightened out. The best liars are those who lie with a good conscience because they themselves firmly believe in what they're saying.

The mist between the houses this morning – like a thin autumn fog. Warm in the house, autumn outside: the rain yesterday evening, it must have been that. A cool wind streams in through the open window: autumn air – I can't help it – autumn air at the beginning of August.

IV

THE CARRELS ON THE AARE – PREMIERES

'We are for the most part more lonely when we go abroad among men than when we stay in our chambers.'

Henry David Thoreau, *Walden: or, Life in the Woods*

1
Overtaking Manoeuvres

Fog too in autumn fifty-eight. From the old Ganter stories back to the Claudia story. Anderson and his stories can wait!

Amthausplatz, Postplatz and through the Obach quarter in the direction of the swimming pool. Or from the opposite side, across the Mutten Levels, past the swimming pool and on to town. After that Gugelhupf treat I was often back in the area around Römerstrasse down there by the Aare.

I'd park my bike by the swimming pool or on Amthausplatz. Then I'd walk around to gather up courage. What would I say if Claudia in her dark jacket and the grey woollen scarf happened to be walking ahead of me and I had to overtake her? How would I address her if she came towards me and I couldn't escape? Autumn fog was as convenient for attack as for retreat, it would be easy to get out of her way in the fog.

Suddenly, early one evening – it must already have been the beginning of November – her casual stride ahead of me, within calling distance. She'd just reached the railway bridge that spans the Aare road. What should I do? Overtake her? First I walked faster, but then I hesitated, followed keeping the same distance between us. All of a sudden I turned off right into Muttenstrasse, broke into a run, turned left into the new path, crossed the stretch of meadow back to Römerstrasse.

Here now, coming towards me through the dusk, was Claudia. There was no time to get my breath, and no time to seek an explanation.

Claudia didn't demand one.

'Oh, it's you,' she said.

A ditherer who's made up his mind, not to do anything grand, perish the thought, but all the same! The privilege of standing alone with the girl on the road. The bliss of finding a third sentence after the first two. And the prospect of a sequel.

On my way back along the same road from which Claudia had just come I sensed a breath of föhn wind over the Aare – in spite of the fog and the cold. Didn't the river banks, the town, look newly washed? Wasn't the air soft and warm in spite of the wet and the cold ? It didn't last long, but I remembered it for a long time as a miraculous sudden change in the weather. And the nagging impatience: what will tomorrow bring?

What exactly was it like at the time? I simply liked it when Claudia was nearby. It didn't matter to me that Bede, Elizabeth, Conrad and Corinne were also there, on the contrary, it made things easier. At school and village theatricals I'd acquired a full repertoire of gestures: stare at someone in an expressive manner and then avert one's gaze, as though distracted by a sign from above; take someone kindly by the shoulder and reason warmly with them; act astonishment or sangfroid, warmth, derision, discontent, displeasure, cockiness, shock, annoyance, fear. But it had never occured to me to use this repertoire except at rehearsals and performances. And when it did occur to me that I could do so in everyday life I didn't dare.

What finally made me ring the Carrels? That overtaking manoeuvre along Muttenstrasse so as to turn up innocently in front of unsuspecting Claudia. Did she really have no suspicion? That was the problem, I couldn't be quite sure. She might easily have seen me as she was crossing Postplatz, one glance in the direction of West Station – that's where I was coming from – and she'd have seen me. The fear that if I didn't do anything I'd be making a fool of myself was greater than the fear of taking the second step.

So it happened that at six o'clock the following evening I was standing in the Furrers' hallway next to the telephone, in my hand a scrap of paper with the number I'd long since learned by heart. Nevertheless I still compared it again with the number in the directory and, for the umpteenth time, repeated the question to myself and decided that it could pass as harmless enough. I'd already seen the film the night before, *Cat on a Hot Tin Roof.* And I'd gone specially to the reading room of the newly opened Central Library: the film had been praised not only in the *Volk* but also in the *Solothurner Zeitung*, ergo it was suitable for an invitation.

The dark oiled wood floor in the Furrers' hallway. Along one wall all kinds of baskets, bins, sacks containing fodder cereal or bran; along the other wall the shelves with the weighing scales and weights, with shoes and rubber boots. Over from the barn the hum of the threshing machine, swelling, subsiding. At this time the year before, I was standing on the improvised platform behind the press, forking the bales of straw up into the hayloft – the bales were pushed in tiny jerks out of the press and along the two beams onto the platform.

The ring of the phone at the other end, insistent, repeated. Then Claudia's voice.

'Oh, yes, that would be nice, why not? I've got enough time,' she said.

She asked what the thudding sound in the background was. I helped her guess.

'Round about eight o'clock in front of the Elite?'

'All right.'

It was that simple.

I paid Frau Furrer for the phone call and remained standing at the kitchen door for a while. We chatted about the wheat harvest the previous summer, about how long the threshing lasted, about the threshing machine. A pity I couldn't help this year, perhaps next year again.

Outside, in front of the barn, the noise of the tractor. Diesel exhaust, dust and chaff swirled around in the cold air.

I'm sure to have gone down to town half an hour too early to buy the tickets, and the Elite wouldn't have been open yet.

I bought balcony seats and took up a position at the foot of the staircase next to the box office. From here I could look out onto the square. People arrived singly, in groups, in pairs. Gradually the Saint George fountain was ringed round by bicycles. Several times I saw someone approaching at a leisurely pace from Postplatz.

Claudia arrived late. I searched for seats in the flickering light of the newsreel.

And two hours later, from the sultry summer heat of South Mississippi back out into the cold town. Wordlessly down Stalden Street and across Postplatz. No Bede here to lead the way, no cues provided. Ask Claudia if she'd liked the film? I couldn't possibly ask her such a fatuous question.

Along the riverside wall something like a conversation got underway. I heard Claudia speak, I heard myself speak. Thrown into the Aare, see if you can swim. *A Streetcar Named Desire, The Rose Tattoo, Baby Doll, The Glass Menagerie* – I'd seen all those films, had seen them several times, and I'd also read the plays. I didn't tell Claudia that I'd been to the Elite the night before to see this most recent film version of a Williams play and form an opinion in advance. Yesterday, on the long way home and half the night, I'd pondered on what to say about it, supposing I dared to invite Claudia and supposing she accepted the invitation. Rich mansions in the American South, death and hysteria and self-deception, Brick's alcoholism and latent homosexuality. Paul Newman acted it all out pretty well, although – Brando would certainly have been better.

Suddenly everything went swimmingly, I'd done enough preparation, the slight headstart helped. I still had something like exam nerves, but that was something I'd learned to cope with long ago.

'Your old Tennessee Williams doesn't spare us anything,' said Claudia, laughing as she spoke.

'Bede would maintain that Williams had read too much Freud,' I said.

'Freud isn't uppermost in Bede's mind any more,' she said. 'He's carrying around another book now: Marx. He puts the little paperback edition down on the desk in front of him for all to see. Bede's most recent reading matter. He always does that. He wants us to know what he's reading. He wants to impress us with his reading. And of course that's exactly what he manages to do.'

The fence, the bushes behind it, the drive down to the garage. We stopped at the garden gate. The light over the front door was on.

Claudia put out her hand, thanked me for the cinema, said, 'Some other time.' She pushed open the garden gate, hurried along to the front-door steps, raised an arm in greeting again and disappeared into the house.

Later, two strips of light beamed out from the basement into the garden, a narrow strip into the black bushes, a wide strip onto the dark lawn. The rest of the house was in darkness.

By the Saint George fountain in front of the Elite mine was the only bicycle left.

2

'Gaudeamus igitur'

'Were you really an active member of that booze brotherhood?'

'Of course I was.'

'And do you still go?'

'Have you ever seen me leave the house in Winznau wearing a student cap?'

'I don't know. Perhaps I missed it.'

'Even if I'd still wanted to – I haven't had a cap any more for ages. However, over all those years I've always paid the annual membership fee, and I still pay it today.'

'So you're still a member of that odd club.'

'Yes, I am, and you're quite right, it really is odd.'

Studentenverbindung is what it was called and what it's still called today, but in spite of their cap-waving carryings-on in pubs and on the street it's only a schoolboy fraternity. There were five *Studentenverbindungen*: In the Amicitia they did gymnastics, in the Arion they sang, in the Palatia they were Catholic, in the Wengia they were initiated into conventional political and economic life, in the Dornachia they were politically neutral, totally geared toward friendship and culture. Gymnastics, singing or liberal democratic politics were out of the question for me, and the Catholic faith didn't mean much to me any more. So all that was left was culture. As I was a model pupil I hardly had a choice anyway. And Bede was a member, that's what finally decided the issue.

Helping out as an actor at evening performances in the village would no longer do. Now I needed to seek friends elsewhere. If I took part in the same activities as Bede and Conrad there was a chance that some time or other Claudia might be around too. During the rehearsals in the summer I'd already found out that both of them knew the Carrels' house from the inside.

At the time, it was normal to be in one of those fraternities. In my own class there was only one student who kept out of it and that was only because he was a promising young forward in the Grenchen football club – it was then the best club in the canton – and what with two evenings' training and the matches at the weekend he didn't have time for anything else.

No, I didn't have anything against those *Studentenverbindungen.* Although later on, after my time at training college, when I was an *Altherr*, an 'elder gentleman', as they called it, I hardly ever went to balls, or the regular *Altherren* meetings or the Saint Nicholas Day drinking sessions, the way many of my fellows did for a long time after. But I paid the membership fee every year and never thought of resigning.

After all, I haven't left the Catholic Church either, although it's more than forty years since I last attended Mass. It's as if I had to remain loyal to whatever was once important to me. A question of loyalty? Hardly. Just not enough determination to say no once and for all to something that had been important to me for a time. As if I didn't want to distance myself from myself – from the person I'd once been.

And would someone like Claudia ever have come to a festival up in Oberdorf, to the fair for example? Would she have strolled through the crowds, in between the stalls with all their bric-a-brac? Perhaps with Corinne. Corinne still knew a few people there, the Weibels had lived in the village for two years. There was dancing in the Kreuz beer garden during the fair: foxtrot, march, tango, slow waltz. If we were to sit down there in the shade of the chestnut trees Corinne would surely be asked to dance. And why not Claudia too, the slender girl in the white blouse and purple skirt? So, Claudia at the fair dance on Assumption Day next year?

But wasn't there already a reason for Corinne and her to come up to the village this year? Once again I'd be acting a farmer's son in the Kreuz hall. Rustic embraces in the footlights. Marriage delayed until the last act because the girl is from a poor family. The appropriate facial expressions would be rehearsed in front of the shaving mirror. A show had to be put on for the people from town: mercenary service abroad with leave-taking and homecoming, call-up of the reserves, the 1798 French invasion. Old schoolmates, whom Corinne also still knew, would shoot me dead on stage: I topple over on my face, gunsmoke billows into the hall while my dying hero's legs twitch, and someone in the wings blows a heartrending tune on the trumpet.

And more of the same.

Things like that had run through my head again and again between the summer and autumn holidays, daydreaming under the trees by the Aare wall, on the Crooked Tower mound, on a bench in the school corridor before the first lesson of the afternoon. It was time to see sense. Undoubtedly Claudia had no interest in candyfloss and roundabouts, she could do without village theatricals.

So I couldn't rely on Oberdorf with its cultural life and social pleasures. If I wanted to go dancing with someone like Claudia there was no getting around the *Studentenverbindung* that organised the appropriate parties in town.

Leapfrogging around the fountain on Marktplatz, new fraternity members horse riding on chairs: 'Gee-up there, I'll teach you manners, you'll see!' A lot of spectators watching from the pavement. The smack of whips on trouser seats, there's no getting out of it, and they giggle and jostle each other, groan too, until the pack arranges itself in a semicircle, cap on head, mouth open: 'In the Black Whale at Ascalon!', many-throated, forte, fortissimo; 'calo, aloh …' echoes down from the house façades, future best citizens celebrating wine, woman and song in Latin.

And then, after the official programme, marching down Hauptgasse in a fivesome, racing down Stalden Street, along the Aare wall and through the railway bridge, caught up, swept along – not alone this time, with others now.

'They're still awake! What did I say? We won't have to strain our throats!' Past the front door and the garage entrance, left around the extension and on into the garden.

Three strips of light on concrete paving and gravel path. Behind us, dark shrubbery and the Aare. Above us, the west wind drove clouds past the moon. And *da capo*, cap on head, mouth open, in the black whale at Ascalon, swallowed up, sent down river, spewed out again.

When we were in the middle of the second verse a curtain was drawn back in one of the windows, the window was opened: 'Well done, wonderful, but that's enough for now, save yourselves the trouble.'

For a brief moment, her slender hand in mine. Claudia wasn't surprised to see me among the singers.

She nodded to me, she nodded to all of us, said something. There I stood, her head only an arm's length from mine. And Barbara, her elder sister, made fun of the boozy din: 'Oh, what a stink of alcohol! Mind you don't light a match!' Nevertheless we were invited in.

In the corner, on the extension side of the house, a large room with level access to the garden; maize mats on the tiled floor, in the rear a corridor leading to other rooms and the stairs up to the house. Herr Carrel had had the whole basement specially converted for his daughters. 'The good thing about the old Carrels is that they seldom show up. People making a noise down here don't disturb those who're sleeping up on the first floor. If there's ever anyone there who wants to sleep.' That's what Bede said some time later.

The leather sofa by the door to the garden, the couch in the rear to the right of the corridor, the wicker chairs, the stools, the high glassed-in bookcase, the walls hung with four-colour prints, posters. And on the couch, on the sofa, on the stools and wicker chairs, and in the corners on the floor: cushions, cushions everywhere, cushions in every colour, bright yellow, pale blue, raspberry red and strawberry red, checked, spotted, flowery, speckled. That was Barbara's hobby, I was told; she found the material at the monthly market or at the bargain counter during sales at Nordmann's.

I'd never met Barbara before. She was already a student, lived in Zurich, but now, on Saturday, she'd come home.

Coffee was offered, various spirits, also wine. Cigarette smoke wafted through the pools of light from the standard lamps. It was good to be seated, to rely on others, to lean back. I sat down on the sofa next to the garden door and listened to what the others were saying, probably I wasn't really listening. I didn't say much myself, hardly said anything. I saw that the others must often have been here before, they knew where the utility room was, where the electric plate for boiling water for the coffee was, they fetched cups without asking, fetched sugar, they knew that the toilet was at the end of the corridor next to the boiler room.

Jacob's performance. He was sitting there lost in thought, his face haggard. They asked him to play something, the house was full of pianos, there was one here too. 'Have you counted the glasses I've drunk? I'll miss half the keys. And that thing here in the basement is out of tune anyway. It wouldn't be fair on Beethoven.' But they didn't relent and in the end he let them drag him onto the piano stool. He began grumpily, but soon he threw back his head and got going.

Was it Beethoven or Bach? I can't remember. Most probably variations, later I often heard him play variations, he always played them with fire and verve. And sometimes, as an encore, he did improvisations with a lot of theatrical hoo-ha.

Jacob too seemed to know his way about the house. He mightn't have been in the same class as Bede and Claudia, and he hadn't taken part in the rehearsals in Lee Forest either, but he was the *cantus magister* in the Dornachia fraternity, and he'd had his first piano lessons from Frau Carrel.

The way Claudia crossed the room, how she turned at the doorpost, dropped down into a corner, stretched out her legs, yawned. The way she listened, didn't listen, raised her head to answer, looked up, looked the other way, shook her earrings. How she bent forward over the ashtray to stub out her cigarette, revealing the neckbones between her collar and her hairline. The way she walked across the floor, over the maize mats, in her socks, in tight drainpipes, in a large, sloppy yellow pullover.

If the others weren't here I wouldn't be sitting here either.

Jacob, sweaty in the armchair, his legs stretched out on a footstool. Now was the time for jazz and chansons, the saxophone, the jingle-jangle of the vibraphone, Juliette Gréco, Edith Piaf, *'Sous le ciel de Paris', 'Je suis comme je suis',* voices from the land of Existentialism. And Bede was there and explained everything.

We didn't break up till long after midnight. On the way out to the garden someone was still telling the final latest joke.

On Amthausplatz I thought of going back to the Aare. But I cycled on. Clouds still swept across the moon, the water in the Aare continued to flow darkly, the house still stood there on the riverbank, with its extension, its roof terrace, its balcony, with the gravel paths, the paving, the walls, the broad strips of light in the shrubbery.

At this hour Langendorf was deserted. Pushing my bike up the slope I worked myself up into a state. A stray dog with puppy-dog eyes, any dog would have been better off, he'd have been able to bark at all the things around him in the November night, at bare trees, façades, street lamps, I wasn't allowed to bark. Outwardly I'd sat there amiably in the din of the pub, downing my beer when challenged, singing when the others sang, gaily taking part in the regimented pleasures. And later on I was just as amiable and inconspicuous among the motley array of cushions, suddenly sitting in a house that for weeks I'd been sneaking around like a lost dog.

Why not admit it, it was the means to an end, that's all. I had no choice but to try to gain a foothold in the town and shake off the village and everything associated with the name of Ganter. Up the slope along the stream, through the cloudy dark, the constant refrain: I'll show them, I'll show them. I didn't know exactly who, I didn't know exactly what.

And what about the Revox? Was it there that evening, somewhere in that big room? I was on the sofa listening to Jacob playing the variations on the piano, I'd never heard him play before. And beside the door to the extension there was that monstrous radio, as big as a chest of drawers, a radio with a built-in record player, and after the variations we listened to jazz, to chansons by Piaf and Gréco. Barbara put on the records. No, she didn't use a tape recorder .

'But, Anna, it's a good thing he's so meticulous. And after all, he's already got his degree.'

'He already had that when I first got to know him. But now he's working on his dissertation as if it had to be goodness knows what: great, authoritative, the longest book ever written by a sinology student in Zurich.'

'Where did he get the idea for his topic?'

'I think it was on his first stay in China. In Zurich, students of Chinese have to go to China for a year, after their foundation course. Even then Benno overdid it – he stayed a year and a half, one semester in Dalian, then in Nanjing where he managed to get a couple of hours teaching German at the university. And there, in Nanjing, a professor told him about that terracotta army: apart from the famous one in Xi'an there were others, including one in their own province, in Xuzhou, only a couple of hours by train from Nanjing. So of course Benno had to set off immediately to see it. I think that's how it all started. Ask him yourself some time, he likes talking about it. Ever since then he goes there for a couple of weeks every year; he meets his supervising professor in Nanjing, then goes on to Xuzhou. That's been going on for three or four years, I think, longer than I've know him in any case. He can't stop, he looks into every detail and keeps finding new documents. I know it's silly of me, but somehow it bothers me to be living with an eternal student.'

'How can you object to thoroughness? Or do you think it's only essential in medicine?'

'Like hell – medicine and thoroughness, you must be joking! But Benno is more scrupulous with regard to his mini terracotta army and anything even remotely connected to it than any doctor in the treatment of his or her patients. A bit excessive and ridiculous when it's only a question of clay fragments, that's what I think. A couple of undeciphered characters more or less – why take it all so seriously? After all, you didn't take ages to finish university, did you?'

'It's not the same. From the very beginning, I'd made a point of getting finished in the shortest time possible – I was always careful to select topics for my semester papers that were easy to narrow down. That way I missed out on a lot of interesting things, and I probably didn't save much time either. No, if that's what interests Benno, let him get on with it.'

Am I too thorough too? No, on the contrary, I'm too lazy. For weeks I've been meaning to find out if anything new has been written about Anderson. I ought at least to look through the last few back issues of the major journals: *American Literature, Modern Language Quarterly, Partisan Review, Jahrbuch für Amerikastudien.* It's something I should have done a long time ago, and I don't even need to go to Zurich for the purpose. I could probably download some of the articles from the internet myself, and where that's not possible the library here can have them sent from other libraries, even from abroad. But I don't get down to it, I postpone it as though I had all the time in the world.

Which I don't have.

Should I start spending my afternoons at the library from now on? Perhaps that would help. Once I'm in the reading room there – with my laptop and a pile of notes in front of me on the table – the semblance of earnestness alone might make me approach my work with greater earnestness.

Anderson and his stories shall wait no longer!

And I'd also get out among people more often.

V

THAT SUMMER – TRILOGY

'… when suddenly one – I know not, but eagerly strive to know, whether it were myself or another, within me or without – said to me …'

Aurelius Augustinus, *Soliloquies*

1
Breaktime Walks

The pale-coloured wheatfield in the shallow depression along the edge of the forest and sloping gently upwards out of the depression and over to the road. Pale yellow with a brownish shimmer. Heads of wheat, tightly packed, bowing slightly on already almost withered stalks, all similar but not quite identical in height, all similarly but not quite identically bowed.

I brushed my hand over them each time I walked along that path. At first they were all still green, a strong bluish green. Then the green grew paler; a shimmer came into the pale green, a shimmer with touches of yellow, of red, of brown.

The vast field, the ears of wheat, coarse-grained, heavy on their slight stems. In dense rows, stem by stem, the wheat stood there, slight in isolation, mighty as a field in the shallow depression along the edge of the forest and all the way up the hill to the road. Absorbing heat, radiating heat, sending a wave of heat towards me as soon as I left the shelter of the forest and took to the footpath.

Yes, a wheatfield, and a barley field, there on the corner of the forest, wheat on my left, barley on my right as I followed the boundary between the two fields up to the road. The smell from the fields shortly before midday, the waves of heat.

I took that path several times a day, always in the same direction from the forest across to the road. I took that path when the wheat was still bluish green, when the green was turning to a yellowy green, again as the yellowy green turned to beige. Soon the reaper-binder would be moving back and forth from the footpath to the road, from the road to the footpath, leaving mowed tracks behind it in the field.

The play of light and shade on the rough carpet of wheat, each head like the other, and yet a little different, living symmetry. Myriad, multitudinous, manifold, both immensely monotonous and immensely varied. The single ear, heavy on its gently bending stalk – and the millions of ears and stalks in the wheatfield here and in the fields of wheat and barley and rye all around.

I can't recall a specific walk, all I remember is the path I took again and again that summer, in June, in July, and also in the first part of August.

Breaktime walks is what I called them.

Breaktime walks through the Furrers' orchard, along the Haselweg as far as the reservoir, from there down the steep footpath to the forest, along the edge of the forest to the group of oak and beech trees at the corner, then on the mud path through the fields over to the road and on as far as the houses on Sagacker Heights and along Langendorfstrasse back to Furrers Farm.

No one I knew would come my way here. None of my teachers lived in Langendorf. Nobody would suddenly turn up on the path and ask me: What about your sore throat? What about that summer flu?

The strange thing was, it was something I never bothered about. The decision to have the flu or something came so easily, it had been the most natural thing in the world. After all, while the others were at their desks down in town, I was also at my little desk out on the landing. Now I got up even earlier than my father, I'd long since eaten my jam sandwiches and was already sitting out on the landing by the time he came out of the kitchen at six and went down the stairs.

As long as school was still on, however, before the summer holidays began, I never went down town, that was something I didn't dare. When I needed a new ribbon for the typewriter my younger sister got it for me. I also never went into the village. My walks on the paths through field and forest were enough exercise.

Only one classmate was in the know after the first few days, Oscar from Langendorf who sat next to me in most of the classes.

One Wednesday afternoon he came by. He knocked at the downstairs door just as I was about to go out on one of my walks. He leaned his arms on the handlebars of his bike and I sat down on the steps.

I see the worn steps, I see the cracks in the wooden wall of the staircase, I see Oscar leaning on the handlebars of his bike, relaxed, as though he'd only dropped in by chance, as if he was in a hurry and had to go off somewhere else right away.

When checking the register the French teacher had asked if anyone knew what was wrong with me. 'And he looked at me,' said Oscar, 'as if I'd be the one to know.

Of course I didn't say anything. I don't know anything, do I? But behind me someone – I think it was Urs – said: What indeed might be wrong with him! And some people laughed as if they knew something, at least that's what it sounded like. So, frankly, what's the matter, are you really ill or are you simply having a holiday?'

I remember the cement floor at the bottom of the stairs, the time of day – it was the middle of the afternoon – the woodpile in front of the house, the weeds in one of the vegetable beds. Oscar would keep me informed. He wouldn't tell on me. And if he did, so what?

No, of course I can't remember the exact place I was at, the night I simply couldn't think up a continuation. It might have been anywhere, didn't I get stuck a dozen times a day!

But this time it was different. It wasn't only for one or two hours that I'd been stumped for ideas: the block had lasted since midday. Again and again I read through the last lines I'd written, read other lines and then others, getting more and more agitated, helpless. Nothing was any good.

I didn't like what I'd written and I didn't see how I could improve it, hadn't the faintest clue. Those sentences in the dialogue I'd just written sounded so wrong, they were so empty, they were so unlike any conversation you might hear in real life! And it was the same with the other dialogues. What was said there was silly, terribly trite or terribly pretentious, without humour or substance, not honest enough, not false enough. The Ganters in the house by the stream talked like Kowalski and Blanche in *A Streetcar Named Desire*, like Willy Loman and Biff in *Death of a Salesman*. Or rather, the way they spoke was completely different: simple-minded, wooden, no one talks like that, not in normal life and not on stage.

How easily I'd always memorised my part in plays, and how rapidly I'd also memorised what each of my opposite actors had to say. But this here was different. And I couldn't do it.

I'd set out to do something I couldn't do, something for which I had not the slightest talent. All the dialogues I'd ever heard or read, the dialogues I'd learned by heart, were of no use to me now. Writing a play was something different, something entirely different from learning a role and then performing on stage. That someone like myself should aspire to write a play was nothing but a bad joke.

And yet I had to do it.

If I only kept on writing and writing and then deleting and deleting, something might yet come of it. But today I hadn't written anything for hours, and all the drafts I'd written so far needed to be deleted too.

It had to be a trilogy, a trilogy of all things! If not a work of intelligence it should at least be long, gigantic – sublimely ridiculous, for all I cared. Claudia, if anyone at all, would be the only person to read it. I had to prove something to Claudia, and to no one else. I'd got myself into this situation. I was right in the middle of it. Now I had to find a way out.

So I remained seated at my table beneath the lamp.

And then I found something to continue with.

Some sentence or other, and I typed it into the machine. Considering that I'd waited a whole afternoon and evening, that sentence would do, at a pinch.

And a single sentence wasn't the end of it, the flow went on, and continued for one, even two whole pages. The sudden feeling of relief was immense, ridiculously so.

Sitting out on the landing beneath the lamp. Everything has come to a standstill. But I don't get up, I don't evade the issue, I don't run away. How easy it would be to give up for the day: I'll find something tomorrow, something will occur to me then, sometime I'll be able to continue. Sometime? In that case it might just as well be now.

Is that the reason why this scene kept coming into my mind later on – not a scene in the play, but the real scene late at night out there on the landing. It fitted in with my former life as a model schoolboy, and it fitted in with what was left in me of that model schoolboy. You started it, so finish it! You mightn't succeed the first time round, nor the second or the third, but that mustn't stop you giving it a fourth try. The very first sentence helped me out, something will always turn up to help you out of your predicament.

That's what I still remembered. The night out there on the landing at the small table beneath the lamp. I'd certainly experienced something similar several times before, but then it had gone by without leaving an impression.

Perseverance in the face of obstacles. All very well when you're writing lousy plays. The silly thing was that I behaved as if perseverance helped in all other cases.

Persevere in love, for example, and your love will be reciprocated – if not today, then tomorrow, if not tomorrow perhaps the day after, definitely in a dozen years. It was the model schoolboy who thought like that. Only a model schoolboy could believe any such thing.

'For you everything goes too slowly, for me everything goes too fast,' I said.

'Too fast? What for example?' Anna asked.

'We've only just had Monday, and now it's already Saturday. I moved in here, temporarily as I thought, the spring before last, and now I'm into my second summer. Days and weeks simply slip past. I've already been stuck here in my retreat, pottering away, for more than a year.'

'There you are, things are moving too slowly for you too. You'd like to get ahead with your Anderson book. And I'd like to get my FMH degree at last.'

'I can understand that. It's nice that you're so impatient. A bit of impatience wouldn't do me any harm either. Over sixty, retired, an old man, it doesn't make any difference any more!'

'That's what you say, it's not what I said.'

'But it's what you thought.'

'No, it's not what I thought either.'

Says Anna, say I, said Anna, said I…

The conversation took place last night. I'm only recording it.

Anna loves arguments like that. And I'm easy to beat.

The trouble I had thinking up dialogues that summer! It wouldn't be any different now.

2
A Little Theory

Once, after the holidays had already started, Oscar, the classmate who'd visited me during my spell of truancy, came by again.

The small table was out on the landing, on the table the typewriter, sheets of paper lay around on the shoe rack and on the floor.

I told him I was writing a play.

He asked me about it.

'You know,' I said, 'writing dialogues is as easy as pie. Of course you have to know the plot of your play, you have to divide up the story into individual scenes, then you have to roughly make up your mind who's talking to whom and about what, and you have to think up what happened before the conversation. Once I've got everything more or less together for the scene, I just stand here – here by the stairs – and take on one of the parts. I put myself into that person's situation and imagine the details, I also imagine the person who'll be on stage with me for the next five minutes and who I'll be talking to. For example I'm talking to a Laura, a Lisa or a Lydia. Yesterday evening at eight, it was a Monday evening, we were supposed to meet in front of the Rex, as agreed. I was there by a quarter to eight. And I waited and waited, but she didn't turn up. So I went to see the film on my own. What shall I say to this Laura, Lisa, Lydia now? Shall I ask her if she'd simply forgotten? Shall I tell her off? Shall I act as though nothing had happened? Shall I apologise for not having a telephone at home so that she had no way of letting me know that she couldn't come? Or should I make fun of the bad film that I went to see all the same? Whatever, I just stand here by the stairs and somehow or other I get going, I start up with something or other and continue, I go on and on talking, I slip into my role, talk as I would in that situation, work myself up into a state of anger, of indignation, I talk myself into making fun of the film and saying how lucky she, Laura, Lisa, Lydia, was not to have been to see it. Well, I let that all go on for a while, and then at some point I say stop, I go over to the table and write down everything I've just said, higgledy-piggledy. Needless to say most of it's rubbish, wide off the mark, it's got nothing or hardly anything to do with the story, it doesn't match the person speaking or the person being spoken to. But that doesn't matter, for the time being anyway. Most of it's tripe, but usually a few sentences can be used after all. All you have to do is give it a good sifting and sorting.'

Thus I delivered my theory.

And I also added where I'd got it from.

'Acting theory, Actor's Studio, famous in New York, the school Marlon Brando and James Dean trained at. Don't act your part, live it. Get totally immersed in the part. Remember your own hopes, your own disappointments, your own desperate waiting. Search within yourself, relive what you've lived through. Live what you act, don't act, live it, that's the main thing. All I've done is adapt the stuff. Why should something that's useful for acting a part not also be useful for writing a part?'

Oscar marvelled.

And it also seemed to make sense to Bede to whom I repeated it at the swimming pool after the summer holidays. 'Oh yes,' he said, 'I see, not bad at all, your little theory. The right thing snitched from the right place, it's as good as making it up yourself.'

At the swimming pool? After the summer holidays? Not only do I clearly remember my conversation with Oscar, my recollection of the one with Bede at the swimming pool is also so vivid that I can hardly doubt that both conversations took place. I can still see the grey wooden sunbeds along the wall, the giant stride, the twinkling water under the diving platform, the alders and the poplars on the banks of the Aare.

I didn't tell Bede how very troublesome it had all been. The little theory I'd pinched from here and there may have served as a writing crutch, but even with the crutch I hobbled along most pitifully.

How often, the winter before, on my way from town up to Oberdorf, the lengthiest of speeches had run through my head! All the things I should have said to Claudia if only they'd occurred to me at the time. All the things I'd tell her next time we met.

But then, the next time I had the chance – and chances were seldom – I realised that none of the prepared speeches really suited the new situation, so I said something else, and on my way home along the Aare, by the time I'd reached the railway bridge, I already knew that I'd said the wrong things once more.

In the dialogues in the trilogy, I could now at last

write down all the things I'd never said. I could write down the things that go through a man's head when he's got a conversation ahead of him that will give his life the decisive turn. Question, answer, questions back, a list of good reasons for this and for that, doubt, confession, criticism of heaven and earth, self-criticism.

That was part two of my little theory.

It was something I never discussed with anyone.

All the monologues that go through the mind of a seeker, a doubter, someone who has been offended, who rails against his fate, who keeps hoping – convert all that inner talk into external dialogue.

Of course I knew that in mundane reality – which was, after all, the real reality – dialogues never worked like that. You start by telling the truth, but then you see astonishment in the face of the woman listening to you, you see incomprehension or even annoyance – and you immediately deviate from what you meant to say, you leave out the question, the reproach, the mocking remark, yes you even leave out the praise. The things your listener says and the expression in her face compel you to temper your words, to be cautious, friendly and kind. The external show never quite follows the internal libretto.

Frank, courageous, caustic: that's what might have distinguished a dialogue on stage from the chatter at the Carrels' garden gate. Which was exactly why you'd want to have your characters talk that way.

Yes, all right, that inner dialogue, written down as it had gone through my head as I cycled home from town, as it ran through my head on my walks to Hazel Wood, past ripening wheat fields early in the morning, along the fields in the shimmering heat of the afternoon, along the pale fields at dusk; all that talk, whipped up out on the landing between the table and the stairs, tested and modified, declaimed to the sound of the rushing stream, the rustling tree tops: whatever all that might or might not have been, at least it was something real; those sentences, flowing, faltering, those beginnings of sentences, those stuttered fragments, had come to me like that, not otherwise, attack and retreat, replies such as would never have occurred to me in the presence of Claudia or Bede; intermingled with things I'd heard at the municipal theatre and seen at the four cinemas in town, things that had impressed me, pale imitations of dialogues I'd heard, films and plays in confusion, a hotchpotch from *A Streetcar Named Desire, On the Waterfront, East of Eden, Requiem for a Nun, Bonjour Tristesse*; a quodlibet with all of those things, lamentation, self-justification, articulated desire, spoken as an aside on the path through the wheatfields, dreadfully chaotic, horribly real, all in the mind of course, anything that came from my mouth was twaddle – if all that been written down, accurately recorded, it might perhaps have been something alive and true.

But of course I wasn't able to write down what went through my mind exactly as it had gone through my mind. Only the smallest part of it found its way onto paper, and then hardly ever in the original order. However long I sorted and rejected, sieved and sifted, there was no wheat there, only chaff, only straw.

No, I wasn't there when the reaper-binder drew its tracks. The next time I passed by, the wheat stooks were already standing in the bare field.

I wasn't there when the stooks were set up; six sheaves at a time, four around a fifth, and the sixth as a cover on top; it was a job I knew, only the year before I'd helped the Furrers with it.

When I went down the path in the early morning I saw the stooks standing in loose rows, an Indian camp in the shallow depression along the edge of the wood and on past the corner of the wood as far as the slope.

One day the stalks are still standing in serried rows, the next day it's a field of stubble, and in the middle of summer, autumn is here with the croaking of crows.

How close they have come again, those weeks in the summer of fifty-nine. I see myself walking through the fields, I see myself over there in the house by the stream, see myself sitting on the landing by the window. The crazy drivel, the crazy scribblings.

Decades later here I am sitting quietly at my iMac trying to show how Anderson's novels, too, are the stories of a storyteller. I proceed step by step, as is to be expected of a retired English teacher. After all, it is to be a serious work, craziness is not what's asked for.

Every two hours I take a break and go on a little walk through the grounds of the Kantonsschule or in the direction of Ypsomed, formerly Autophon. And in the afternoons I work in the reading room of the Central Library.

At last I've got to the stage where I can take a look at a few other authors who've written about American small-town life and the life of ordinary people in the smaller and larger towns of New England or the Midwest. I've only just realised that Sinclair is one of them. He portrays the provinces and their inhabitants in several novels besides *Main Street* and *Babbitt.*

I read and read. Some things get sent to me from other libraries, some I order from Lüthy's bookshop. And the week before last, Erica brought me a parcel of books from Edinburgh. She finds books for me in London and Edinburgh, while I go to Winznau from time to time and make sure that the roses don't dry up.

It's ridiculous of me to pretend to my daughter that I'm lazy whereas I keep at my work day in, day out. On the other hand it's true that my progress is very slow. Anna tells me that Benno is flying to China again at the end of August, and she makes fun of him because once again he'll be chasing after fragments of his terracotta army. Anna could also make fun of me. One small town more or less is of no account, but pedantry and small-town life belong together!

And what else happened these last few weeks? Anything worth reporting? I probably won't find out what's been going on in American small towns this summer before I read a new novel by Roth or Updike in three of four years time. The Americans will be voting in the autumn, and a senate committee has just found out that the government hyped up the CIA reports: there were no weapons of mass destruction in Iraq, nor was Saddam working with al-Qaeda. I bet that will hardly stop the Americans from electing Bush again. After all, the man introduced democracy to Iraq and Afghanistan, all the rest is peanuts, including Abu Ghraib and Guantanamo and the Valerie Plame affair. And the fact that it's apparently all the same to Bush and the majority of voters whether or not Israel continues to erect its great wall against the barbarians: that's peanuts too!

VI

SHAME AND PRIDE

'He had a good dream. It's the only dream you can have – to come out number-one man.'

Arthur Miller, *Death of a Salesman*

1
'Hey, you there!'

A simple *Kneipe* beer party or a formal *commercium*? It must have been a *commercium,* the Saint Nicholas Day meeting in December fifty-eight: formal, with a lot of 'elder gentlemen', with speeches, singing and various 'productions'. I myself was also asked to provide a 'production', it was my first, a theatrical performance of course, the Hamlet soliloquy in an exaggeratedly theatrical style. A few weeks before, I'd heard the actor Moissi on the radio, a historical recording, and now I was trying to do something in the same style, in a solemn, high-pitched voice, drawing out the vowels into tremolos, it was to be a caricature, and funny as befitted the occasion.

Generally my father limited his visits to the Oberdorf and Langendorf pubs. He didn't know many people in town and he'd never liked sitting alone at a table without a few friends around him. I could be almost sure I'd never meet him in a pub in town.

Until that Saturday evening when I found him sitting in the Roter Turm.

I spotted him just as I was on my way to join my friends. We'd decided to wait for each other in the room down here before going up to the formal meeting in the big room upstairs. Jacob and a few of the others were already there, seated at the regulars' table against the wall on the right. Just before I reached them I saw my father sitting over in the corner, I saw him from a distance and from the side only: I saw him raise his beer bottle while another man talked at him across the table.

Just in time I managed to turn round. With my back to him I remained standing for a moment. 'I've forgotten something, I'll be back in a minute,' I told Jacob, and headed off towards the bar and the exit.

But I'd hardly gone two paces in that direction when I heard someone call out behind me:

'Hey, you there!'

It made me turn my head towards the corner I'd been trying to avoid. He'd risen halfway from his chair, supporting himself on the table with one arm as he waved the other.

'Hey, you there, hey!'

There were a lot of people in the Roter Turm at the time, most of the tables were taken and new people kept coming in, causing a congestion near the bar as they looked around for spare seats.

Once outside, I tried to persuade myself that my father hadn't realised that I'd seen and recognised him. I tried to persuade myself that he'd have put it down to my absent-mindedness that, although I'd looked back, I'd simply gone away, apparently imagining it had been somebody else calling someone else. I told myself that he couldn't hold it against me. I told myself that he must have told himself that he'd probably been mistaken.

Going back to the pub was out of the question. He'd be sure to come over to our table. And if he didn't come, I'd be the one who'd have to go over to his table – after all I couldn't pretend I didn't recognise him, not again. Back out on the street, I still felt shaken.

My father hadn't come home at midday, he hadn't come home for supper either. That was something we were used to, it was normal. And it was also normal that when he came home late he was most often in an unpredictable mood, either extremely cheerful or extremely rancorous. That didn't bother anyone in the house by the stream. But a presentation of that old performance to my new friends here in town! That's what I'd recoiled from, I didn't want to be a spectator of that play, I didn't want to have a part in it.

Later I used it for a scene in the trilogy. The 'Hey, you there!' scene is one of four pub scenes. When I was still a child I was sometimes sent to look for my father up in the village, and when I finally found him he usually ordered a glass of apple juice for me. In those days I quite liked sitting beside my father in the Kreuz, the Engel, the Sternen or the Helvetia, in those days I didn't feel at all ill at ease in the noise and the cigarette smoke.

But what was to be done now? I couldn't possibly go back to the others down in the pub. And even if I went straight up to the room where the meeting was to be held I was in danger of bumping into my father. He'd be sure to be coming out the very moment I was going through the entrance or had only just reached the foot of the stairs. It would be all right if he was alone. Ah, it's you. Since when have you started patronising this posh pub? Who dragged you here? Something would be bound to occur to me. Really, it was childish the way I'd behaved, and cowardly to boot.

I went down the Hauptgasse towards Stalden. At the Elite Cinema I turned back: Why should I let such a trifling matter spoil my evening. So, back to the Roter Turm.

I reached the upstairs room unmolested. Most of them were already there. The party began: 'For praiseworthy doings we're now gathered here, So, brothers, sing Ergo bibamus!' I behaved as the others behaved, did what the others did, drank when I had to, joined in when someone proposed a drink, drank three or four glasses of beer without being thirsty, all so as to forget the beckoning arm. I'd seen the arm beckoning to me, I'd seen the face.

And I was annoyed to be here. Why did I have to drink a quarter or half glass simply because Jacob at the other end of the table raised his arm to drink my health and himself drank up a half or quarter glass. Why did beer-drinking have to be regimented? What was so special about it to make it a question of etiquette? What was the whole show for?

'Folklore,' said Bede beside me and nodded breezily. 'A show, you're right, that's exactly what it is. Boy's stuff for men. I play along because Papa played along. For a change I too want to play along where others play along, where everyone else is playing along. I want to be a sheep in the flock. I want to bleat. I want to be shorn. It's only right and proper. It's part of our little town. We all need a bit of fun.'

That evening I was annoyed to be sitting in the Roter Turm. Yet later on I often sat there, or elsewhere, playing my part in the 'Ah, student glory in days of yore' melo. This glory was celebrated again and again, joyfully, vigorously, in the Roter Turm, in the Krone, in the Cardinal across the river, once in the Wengistein, beer parties, *Commers* gatherings, anniversary parties, *Totensalamander.*

Yes, *Totensalamander* too, ceremonies commemorating former Kantonsschule pupils who'd gone on to become university students and then engineers, doctors, directors, department heads and bosses. After becoming an 'elder gentleman' at the age of nineteen or twenty, straight after the Matura, one remained an 'elder gentleman' all one's life, and as such was duly honoured once more, after one's death, with speech, toast and song. I've always had a soft spot for those funeral rites in our meeting room: the melancholy in the midst of youth, memento mori. The life stories I heard there moved me.

That evening at the Roter Turm, however, I didn't feel anything of the sort, my only feeling was one of uneasiness. Probably my father was still sitting down there in the pub. It might easily occur to him or to his companion to go and see what all that student noise was about, pure curiosity, and suddenly Ganter would be standing at the door of the room. 'Hey, you there, hey!' He was quite capable of such a thing, he'd never been afraid of people.

All that evening I was scared he might suddenly turn up. And I even feared the end of the evening, was afraid he might bump into me as I left. I was annoyed with him,

123

and I was annoyed with myself, annoyed that I was sitting in the midst of that loud jolly crowd, annoyed with the others who could get drunk with an easy conscience, and then on Monday they'd boast how well they could carry their drink or how long it had taken them to sleep it off.

'Good form and manners? Don't make me laugh,' said Bede. 'As if it ever depended on that! It's nothing but a question of what rung of the ladder you're standing on. If you're at the bottom you need manners simply in order to preserve a necessary degree of self-esteem.'

No, Claudia's mother would never have shown up in the Roter Turm like my father. Even at home she retreated to the upper floor. Visitors to the Carrels' house could only guess at the suffering that took place there. The Carrels' good reputation did not suffer. Whereas Ganter's fortnightly drunken homecomings with his reduced paypacket were notorious throughout the village.

'She suits you,' Bede once said. 'You two match.' He did not say why we matched. Your old man and Frau Carrel, he could have said, both have the same problem. But he never said anything of the kind, he didn't even drop a hint.

Up to her marriage Frau Carrel had performed as a concert pianist. Then the children, Barbara and Claudia, came. Her career suffered, from now on she only played chamber music. And there were regular house concerts in the house on the Aare. Besides that, there were the piano lessons she gave a few selected schoolgirls and boys. And then, somehow or other, the sweet liqueurs and the white wine must have come into it.

It was only years later that Claudia admitted that the rumours were true, and also that Papa Carrel didn't worry too much if her mother stayed away for a couple of days when she was in a crisis period.

In such a household the daughters were left more or less to their own devices. They didn't give any trouble: their pocket money was control enough. That's why you could go there after every beer party – and at any other time too. That's why, as a rule, no one up in the house was disturbed by the noise from the loudspeakers down in the basement and in the annexe. That's why the supplies of gin, whisky, cognac and wine were always refurbished. The Carrels had other cares.

We might have compared what could be compared – if only because of the differences. But we never talked about it. Only once, much later, did it come up. Usually a conversation gets into swing once you've started talking. But Claudia remained monosyllabic, dismissive, unapproachable. I did all the talking. Her family problems and mine did not cancel each other out on a higher plane.

2
'Oh to get away! To some place else!'

Of course I'd seen from the start that there was a difference beween the Carrels on the Aare and the Ganters by the stream. But when did I become fully aware of that difference, aware of it in an increasingly embarrassing way? As early as the summer holidays? Not till after the autumn holidays?

I never talked about my family to my new friends. Why should I have mentioned the Ganters by the stream to them of all people? The house by the stream was the house by the stream, I was used to living there. I was kept busy with gathering wood in Lee Forest and up in the gorge, digging up the garden, doing the weeding, feeding the rabbits. On top of that there was the work at Furrers farm: haymaking, harvesting, picking up potatoes, pulling up turnips. Since starting at the training college, however, I only seldom went to help the Furrers; instead, I worked on building sites in the holidays.

Most often we were short of money. The clothes we wore always had to be cheap. My mother did a lot of dressmaking herself: skirts, dresses, blouses for my sisters. She altered trousers for me and my father. Once – I was still at the secondary school – I bought a pair of second-hand shoes I'd seen advertised in *Schweizer Jugend*. Once, my mother made me a jacket out of an old raincoat. Once, I had to break open my little steel money-box to take out the sum I needed for a school outing to Bern.

Of course, I'd also occasionally felt ashamed before. I'd felt ashamed when I had to go and fetch my father in the Kreuz, in the Helvetia or in the Engel, I'd felt ashamed when my father arrived late at play rehearsals – and yet at the rehearsals in particular there were enough occasions when I could be proud of him.

It didn't bother me when the Furrers and other neighbours came to see us. Since my mother did all kinds of sewing work, women from the village often came to our home. And men came by to ask my father to do this or that little masonry job. Members of the Mixed Choir came by. I quite enjoyed it when we had visitors.

But Claudia, Claudia in our kitchen? Out of the question, quite impossible! Claudia should not be allowed to know what the place looked like. The old wood-burning stove, the gas ring on the stand in the corner, the two cupboards – I'd painted them years ago during the height of my model pupil phase – the kitchen sink, the table, the stools: Claudia should not be allowed to see all that. She should not see the earth closet, nor my den by the window in the attic, she wasn't to know that in summer I slept out on the landing, in winter in the living-room.

At the same time I knew perfectly well that there were several such houses in the village, I'd been in other kitchens and living rooms often enough, whenever my father took me with him to collect the trade union dues. Those entrance halls, kitchens and sitting rooms didn't look very different to ours. And here too there were cursing men, nagging women. In every house there was something to be ashamed of, slightly ashamed at least.

But that didn't count any more.

Ever since the rehearsals in Lee Forest, ever since those long walks along the Aare, the night walks through the Obach quarter, something had changed. Claudia with her fun-loving friend Elizabeth, Bede who – for whatever reason – liked me, Jacob with his piano-playing. Their world and my world – the difference was striking. I saw nothing but differences. And all the old stories came back again, the long series of small humiliations – I'd pushed them aside.

Was it shame, rebellion, hurt pride? Was it something else? Not only had I started to loathe my own family, I must also have started to loathe myself. I was in the wrong place and I hadn't noticed that I'd been in the wrong place all the time.

3

'Catch me if you can!'

'What! You're reading Anderson? Since when?'

'Well I have to, don't I? After all I'd like to know what you're working on, what's been keeping you busy for such a long time. Dr Reefy, the one with the young wife, the paper pills and the gnarled apples, he's the one I like best. But what I wanted to ask you: George Willard, you know, the young newspaper reporter, he has a role in several of the stories and in the end he leaves the small town, is he the reason you named my little brother George? It's not really a very common name, you must have got the idea from somewhere.'

'You really think we went through all of American literature in search of something suitable? If you like, there's no simpler way, is there? On the other hand Erica's grandfather was also named George and there are several other Georges in her family, don't ask me why. It's the same with the Ganters, dozens of Pauls. However, it's a nice coincidence that George is the namesake of George Willard.'

'What about Anna, what made you come up with Anna, what gave you the idea for my name?'

At my very first beer party I was asked if I had any sisters. It was a friendly question. Boys who had sisters provided their fellows with an additional opportunity to invite a girl to a Dornachia fraternity dance, either to the big ball in the winter or to one of the so-called *Kränzchen*; there was always a demand for information about any new girls who could be invited.

I couldn't deny that I had two sisters: Corinne – who had been my classmate in Oberdorf before her parents moved to the town – was sure to remember how Katherine, years ago, had provided a show of bad school conduct.

Originally, Katherine had passed the entrance exam to the regional secondary school in Langendorf. But after the trial period she was sent back to the village school. Maybe she hadn't worked hard enough for school, maybe she'd spent too many of her free afternoons helping out at the Furrers'.

Whatever the reason, she was sent down, so that after the summer holidays she was back with those who'd failed the exam in spring, she was sitting with those who were unlikely ever to get a proper apprenticeship and who'd finish up doing piece-work in a factory, she was back in grade seven and she behaved as if this school had nothing to do with her, as if school in general had nothing to do with her.

If she'd been given two hours to write an essay in class, she'd hand in exactly four lines at the end saying she hadn't had any ideas. When all the others did pencil drawings of their deskmate's head, she covered her drawing paper with red doodles of Indian heads in feathered war bonnets. When they had to do the sums as far as exercise ten, she stopped at exercise six or continued on to exercise twenty. When they were all gathered in a semi-circle around the harmonium she purposely sang out of tune. Not a week went by when she wasn't made to change her place for bad behaviour, either to the row directly in front of the teacher's desk or else to the back row. On one of those disciplinary transfers she put on a great show of moving all her things, only to sit down at her old place again after the recreation, just as if nothing had happened.

Herr Joller, the teacher, was otherwise a good-natured person. But Katherine made him lose his patience. He gave her more and more lines each time. He raised his voice, he made threats, he pounded the desk with his fist.

Once while he was writing on the board, his back to us, something smacked against the wall up in front, and then again, this time near the chalk writing, loud and clear. We all kept still, poker-faced, no one said anything. But Herr Joller had hardly turned back to the blackboard when someone in the front row was already spitting on her blotting paper and moulding it into fresh ammunition. It skimmed past Joller's arm and smacked onto the board right into the middle of the writing. Once doesn't count, twice can be a coincidence, but now Katherine was caught; she ducked down over her desk, covering the paper scraps with her hands.

At that time I was in grade five. Herr Joller taught grades five and six as well as the upper grades; it was the only time I had the same classroom as my sister.

Before that, Katherine's behaviour had never attracted attention. She'd always found learning easier than I or my younger sister. She'd never needed to be hard-working, she'd never had to spend much time on her homework. She'd always been an unremarkable pupil who'd had good marks in her reports. Now all of a sudden she was a poor student, and one who never missed an opportunity to attract attention. As if she'd said to herself: if I was too dumb to stay on at the regional secondary school, I might as well act really dumb now.

Straight across the square in front of the school building, black cassock chasing red frock. Past the fountain, across the square and on under the lime trees, down the slope and off right, into Engelweg, the priest. Ahead of him Katherine in her red frock, turning her head from time to time to see if she still needed to run. There was no need to run any more; halfway between Kirchrain and the chaplaincy the priest stopped, remained standing there for a moment, then turned back. As he came back up Kirchrain we saw him wipe the sweat from his face with the back of his hand, then mop it dry with his handkerchief. We all moved back from the windows to our desks. Footsteps on the stairs; from the door, that had remained open all the time, the priest cast his eye over the class. Arms folded, silence. He sent us all home.

She'd stuck out her tongue at him. She hadn't given him any answers. She'd refused to stand up when she'd been summoned. She might at least stand up, he'd said. But she'd remained seated. He'd had to say it three times. Then, at the third summonings she'd leant across her desk as if she were glued to the chair and had stuck out her tongue at him. I myself, in the back of the room with the other fifth grade pupils, hadn't seen it, but the others claimed afterwards that that was what had happened. But probably the priest hadn't noticed it either. For all he did was send her out of the room, as he'd done before, as he'd often done. The ten plagues one after the other in rapid succession, little Moses being rocked in the basket, then grown to manhood. The priest was in the middle of the story when there was a knocking at the door. Outside in the corridor no one but Katherine, and he asked her if anyone had been there, he thought he'd heard someone knock. And then he was back at his desk and went on with the story about Moses the man, about Pharaoh and about the brazen serpent, until suddenly there was another knock at the door, loud now so that everyone heard it. And as he opened the door and stepped out into the corridor we heard a pitter-patter down the stairs: catch me if you can! – The religious instruction lesson would have been over soon anyway. He'd come by in the evening, he said.

It was the only time the priest came to our house. My father wasn't at home. Rita and I were sent out of the living-room. The priest didn't stay long. The Ganters by the stream were not particularly receptive to pastoral care.

'What business did that man have coming here?' my father asked the following evening. Then: 'Go and apologise at the presbytery. I never want to see that coalbag here again, do you hear?'

I tried to make the best of a bad job. When I was asked catechism questions I gave the answers word for word, including what was in the small print. I put up my hand eagerly. I no longer ever skipped Thursday early morning mass before school.

That Katherine had put her tongue out at the priest remained a rumour. And she went no further: she answered back, she grumbled, she was defiant, she didn't improve nor did she get worse. Then, as the entrance exams for the regional secondary school approached Katherine changed slightly. She'd give it another try.

Although she'd acted the idiot for almost a year she passed the exam, she also passed the probationary period. This time she scraped through.

4

Model Pupil

I'd always been a quiet boy at school, but at that time I was not yet a model pupil. It must have started when Katherine suddenly began to attract attention because of her bad behaviour – with me in the fifth and she in the seventh grade and both of us in the same classroom with the same teacher. The whole village knew all about Ganter's pub crawls, his diatribes, his torrents of invective and derision. Now the whole village also knew all about Ganter's cheeky daughter. I'd been used to the one, now the other caught me unawares. I had to show my teacher, Herr Joller, that there was someone in the Ganter family who was different, completely different.

It was no longer enough simply to be quiet and modest and polite. It was no longer enough to learn ballads off by heart and recite them flawlessly, loud and clear. And it was not enough to be more obedient and diligent than Katherine, I now had to be better than all the others, I had to be a paragon of diligence and obedience. It hadn't been planned, it was not something I'd decided, it just came about.

My zeal might have waned after I'd reached grade six and my sister was no longer in the same classroom compelling me every day to impress everyone with my exemplary behaviour. Perhaps I might have slackened in my frenzied zeal to counter the Ganters' bad reputation.

My bad habit was the second decisive incentive. In grade five it was shame at Katherine's public conduct, in grade six it was shame at my own secret sins.

I see the bean patch, I see the two rows of bush beans, the cauliflower patch, the blackcurrant bushes. I'm the boy who picks beans in the garden on his afternoons off, who can be depended on to do the jobs assigned to him by his mother, who is ready to do anything to help the household out of its precarious condition. And in the evening Mother will cook the beans and I'll help her string them on threads, and then we'll hang up those garlands of beans in the attic between the rafters. Dried green beans for the winter.

The beans, the foliage, the cauliflower patch. It must have been late summer, towards the end of August, grade six. None of my sisters around, neither Katherine nor Ruth, but I'm not on my own there, bent over on the garden path picking beans. Kurt is crouching next to me. 'And afterwards you have to string them too? What a dope! That's girl's work. I've got a better idea.' And he picks up a head of cauliflower.

'What do you want that for?' I ask in astonishment. But he's already picked up a second cauliflower and with one slash of his pocket knife he's cut off the stalk. 'Don't act so dumb, I'll show you something, just guess what!' With a smirk he chops off the leaves with his knife. Then out through the garden gate over to the stream and into the old henhouse, secretively, and always ahead of me, as if he was the one who lived here, I in his wake, hesitant yet curious about what's to follow. And in the semi-darkness of the henhouse there he is, sprawled out on the pile of hay in the back corner. 'And now, take a good look, here's something I bet you've never thought of!' Already he's shoved one of the heads of cauliflower up under his shirt, high up in front of his collarbone. 'Not bad, eh?' he asks, and immediately places the other cauliflower next to it. 'With this I'd be a match for Katherine, don't you think?' He giggles, grins. 'Why don't you go and fetch her bra?' And while I turn red and feel embarrassed and say 'Are you mad?' and make to leave, he drops the cauliflowers and takes a grab at my shorts leg. 'Show us, let's have a look!' He crouches down and takes a look. 'You'll have to confess that. Your own fault if you're a Catholic.'

Anything can give rise to a bad habit. If Kurt Meier, who was a protestant, hadn't threatened me with the priest, it would probably never have occurred to me that there was anything wrong with my new pleasure. Have I entertained impure thoughts? Been guilty of impure actions? Alone or with others?

In the end it wasn't the 'examination of conscience' in the catechism that set me back on the right path. Three volumes on the human being that I found in the attic in the autumn impressed me more than the corresponding list of sins in the catechism. More than two thousand pages of scientific information on yellowed paper, black and white illustrations, and a man and a woman in full colour on glossy card paper inserted in the back of the book; the abdominal wall, the chest, and the back of the head could be folded out; if you took away, one after the other, the lungs, the heart, the stomach, the liver, the intestines, the kidneys, you saw parts of ribs in bright yellow against the deep red flesh; nerve nets, the lymphatic system, each of the glands separately, the blood circulation, everything in accordance with the state of knowledge at the turn of the century; one volume on natural healing, one volume on the history of morality, on marriage, education and hygiene down to the last incomprehensible detail. Here I received enlightenment from a reliable source about what I was doing with a beginner's enthusiasm in the henhouse, in the Furrers' shed behind the apple pomace barrels, under the hazel bushes by the stream, often alone, seldom with others. There, in black on white, something I could never have found out for myself, together with all the dire consequences. Outbreak of sweating by the window up in the attic. I skimmed through the pages, leafed back, reread – never had a textbook, never had a subject been ploughed through with such avidity, with such apprehension: I was on the sure path to creeping neurasthenia, to full dementia.

Looking in the mirror I found confirmation of what I'd feared: The vice was already reflected in the greenish shadow under my eyes, the sickly pallor shimmering through the summer tan on my face. If I stretched out an arm, incipient spinal marrow atrophy already brought on finger tremors. My lack of concentration. The pressure in my lower back. The emptiness in my head. If I hadn't come across those books, everything would soon have been over for me without my realising. The fact that the previous tenant of the house, a long-deceased uncle of the Furrers, had left those books behind in a box in the attic was a sure sign from above. A sign of mercy, an offer of rescue in the nick of time.

'Nice that the rest of us don't have to wash ourselves any more,' said Katherine. 'He washes enough for the whole family.' Twice daily from head to foot, in cold water of course: in the morning just a quick splash with water, down in the wash house; before bedtime, a thorough wash with soap at the kitchen sink upstairs. The book prescribed a strict course of treatment, to be carried out with love, understanding, patience. Any stimulation was to be shunned. Even the most fleeting sensual imaginings were to be brushed aside, instantly.

Endurance runs up to Hazel Wood, endurance runs along the stream. Every free afternoon occupied with farmwork for the Furrers or gathering wood up on the mountain for the winter. After supper, after I'd finished my regular homework, I learned the catechism off by heart, or I did all the sums in my maths book once again from beginning to end, or copied whole pages out of the dictionary, studied all kinds of complicated spelling rules.

However, by Christmas there'd been absolutely no improvement, in fact my vice had grown even stronger instead of weaker, a protracted evil and no end in sight. All that was improving was my reputation as a model schoolboy.

In order to keep up my physical strength at least, I ate twice as much as before. I stuffed myself with bread, potatoes, rice pudding and apple puree, so that after every meal my stomach felt loaded and my head queasy. My mother took note of my good appetite with ill humour, there was seldom anything left over any more for her to heat up.

Try to think of other things, decent, healthy, clean things. At the same time keep yourself incessantly busy with something or other: a hurried prayer or spelling practice, sums or catechism questions. Litanies of penitence on the way through Hazel Wood, ardent remorse, this is the last time, never again, not even once; the innumerable second last times, last times, absolutely last times. On the path through the woods I renewed my old resolutions, a private matter between the Lord and me. The only person I called on to intercede on my behalf was the Virgin Mary: in such intimate company I didn't need to feel ashamed. If she helps me for five days I'll give her a completely sin-free sixth day for good measure – and to prove it I will now smash this beech branch, which is as thick as my arm, against the trunk of a fir tree so that it breaks in two, then hurl the pieces into the blackberry bushes. And that's how I'll break with my past life, I'll fling it away. In a week, when I'm back here at the crossing, everything will be completely different.

You have to cut down nettles before they flower, but even then they spread, they manage to survive in the poorest of soils, they're tough weeds. Aided by the advice in pious sex education books, and with my weekly penitential pilgrimages through Hazel Wood, stumbling and rising and stumbling again I got myself on the right path.

My good habits were still prone to disruption. That's why I remained on my guard. I continued to sublimate for all I was worth, and was by no means choosy – I took whatever was set before me, relished it. I could no longer go to bed without a textbook, I swotted up one paragraph after the other until I fell asleep over the book; and on waking up I immediately reached out for my maths book to find the difficult sum I'd picked out the evening before. I knew all about Ancient Egypt, the Hellenes in Hellas, the Roman Empire, the migration of peoples, about emperors and popes, I could supply information about prehistoric animals, zoophytes and molluscs, invertebrates and vertebrates, about cell structure, Ethiopia, gasworks, turbines, rocket technology.

At the secondary school in Langendorf I was now fortunate enough to have a model teacher, a man who gave due credit for perfect presentations of written work, who set regular and frequent tests and made us stand to attention at the start of PT lessons. These strictures were made-to-measure for young Ganter. We were marched through the material at a military pace. Even in homework the geometric figures had to be traced with Indian ink in three colours.

And on the first Sunday of every month I set up broad guidelines of conduct. In a notebook bought specially for the purpose at Nordmann's, I listed, in order of priority, all the things I'd have to pay particular attention to in the following four weeks – frugality in sleep and food, for example, followed by French and Geometry. Then I set out the schedule for the coming week: when to get up in the morning, when to go to bed, when to perform my tasks in house and garden, when and what I'd learn for school, when and what I'd read in addition and alongside the rest. And finally, on a sheet of paper, the agenda for the following day: each quarter of an hour programmed in advance, the time allowed for shoe-cleaning as precisely defined as the subject to be pondered over on the way to school, on those empty stretches between Oberdorf and Langendorf.

First work, then pleasure, you have to keep a balance. For things to go well, you have to let go from time to time, it's the only way to achieve a stable character. I took that in hand too: I prescribed myself the occasional chat with schoolmates in front of the dairy, organised excursions to the swimming pool in summer, went skiing on the Weissenstein in winter, went on a one-day cycling tour with Ernst Furrer in spring, and, long before I'd reached the required age, granted myself Sunday afternoon visits to the cinema to see *The Robe* or *The Living Desert*.

I must have felt real pleasure in giving myself orders and then obeying them. Visible activities were not the only thing I prescribed; my thoughts and feelings too had to conform to my will and plan. And before falling asleep I ticked everything off: finished, done, behaviour satisfactory, should do still better. Each day was made up of an elaborate succession of exercises in virtue, wagers against my self, proofs of achievement, tests; and whenever I didn't pass, the same thing was put on the schedule for the following day – the dictatorship of morality, Holy Mary, place your foot on the Jura viper, with diligence, order and cleanliness things are sure to improve, in the long run failure is impossible.

This regimented life led me to feel superior to my classmates, and years ahead of them. At the same time I told myself that it would be arrogant to show my superiority and that, on the contrary, modesty and discreetness would be more becoming. So that's how I tried to behave, I did what I had to do secretly, always in the knowledge that I'd earned the right to feel comfortable in my skin.

Did I really feel comfortable? Life as an obstacle race: I clambered, I leaped, I crawled, I sweated and panted, I exhausted my powers. What did I care about epidermis, dermis, hypodermis, stratum corneum, mucous membrane, cross-sections in the textbook? It was all only so that I could put up my hand, dry up my pen, and get good marks in my spring and autumn end of term reports.

This lasted for almost four years. In spite of initial difficulties and relapses I got through prepuberty and puberty in much the same way as the virtuous lads in the books in the Oberdorf parish library.

'That rascally face. He lied to them, and now they've elected him again! He's convinced he's in direct personal contact with God, and he believes in his crusade against the rogue states.'

'Calm down,' says Anna. 'Do you really think things would be different with someone like Kerry?'

'Probably not, admittedly. The Americans are very good at electing peculiar presidents. Really, they've managed splendidly with Bush Junior. The goodies and the baddies, there's nothing in between. Whoever is not for me is against me, ergo a rogue. And the idea that their own country might also be a rogue state is something that could never occur to them.'

'Hey, keep your hair on!'

'Why should I? Why not let me get in a flap about America and the Americans? I only get annoyed at them because they absolutely refuse to live up to the high opinion I had of them for such a long time. Babitt and Rabbit and Ishmael and George Willard and Wing Biddlebaum and Reefy and – don't look so surprised! – Zuckerman, you know, they're really not bad people, estimable and, in my view at least, far more likeable than Bush and Co. That lopsided, rascally grin! But apparently it's the kind of simple-minded charm that appeals to a majority. It would've been better if the man had stuck to alcohol and if his visions came from whisky and not from up above. But what of it, possibly his pious friend Blair's belief in his own lies is even stronger.'

'What have you got against him? After all he's your comrade, so to speak.'

'So to speak – well said! To be honest, I'd do better to fume at him, I'd have even more valid reason. What a cuckoo in the Labour Party nest!'

'Bush and Blair, the only ones still missing are Berlusconi and Blocher.'

'And on to political smalltalk! You're right to make fun of me. Why get annoyed? It's no use, has no effect, not even the slightest. I might just as well pray to the Virgin Mary for a just peace in the Holy Land.'

'And does that make you depressed?'

'Why? Should it? Okay, perhaps it should. Not depressed, not outraged and not angry, no big feelings, it's just sufficent to make me feel annoyed, always enough for that, for so much at least. Read the *New Statesman* and the *WochenZeitung,* listen to the BBC and, every day, to *Echo der Zeit.* You know such a lot and could know a hundred times more. But there's nothing you can do. Not absolutely nothing, but hardly anything. Dutifully take part in referendums and elections, usually lose, but nevertheless go and vote again the next time.'

'That sounds rather tame.'

'So it is. Tame and dutiful, as behoves a model citizen.'

VII

GREAT EXPECTATIONS

'… he was afraid that if he sat down he would fall into the odd detached kind of stupor in which he had spent so large a part of his life …'

Sherwood Anderson, *Poor White*

1
'Mr Smith is a Man'

'Mr Smith is a man. Mrs Smith is a woman. John is a boy. Helen is a girl. The baby is also a girl. Mr Smith is the father. Mrs Smith is the mother …' Above the text, simple line drawings of a man, a woman, a boy, a girl, a baby. That's how the course began. The family, the parents, the children. That's how I learned English.

Did the correspondence course cost six or seven francs a month? I only know that the booklets arrived regularly at the end of the month, cash on delivery. I paid for the course with the money I earned at the Furrers'. And if for once I didn't have enough money, my mother will have paid for me, grudgingly of course, but she couldn't be seriously opposed to my learning English.

English by the Nature Method. The course lasted sixteen months, a booklet a month, with four chapters in each booklet. According to the instructions, students should devote half an hour a day to study; the main task being to read a story. Not just short texts like those in the French textbook at school but complete stories, without any translation, exclusively in English from the start, but always such that if I read the new chapter carefully I could guess the meaning of the new words and sentences with the help of the words I already knew. 'Mr Smith is a man. Mrs Smith is a woman …' was easy to understand with the help of the pictures. And so it continued, one thing following from the other in tiny steps.

In the letter accompanying the first booklet you were told to read the text out loud three times each day. And when I'd thus memorised the new instalment of the story I could do the exercises and then send them in for correction. In the first exercise of each of the four chapters you had to fit single words into sentences, but in the second one you had to answer questions. In later chapters you had to write your own texts, little compositions in your own English. The exercises were always promptly returned, with corrections and encouraging remarks.

I got up at the same time as my father. So I had plenty of time for my English every morning before setting off for school in Langendorf. I still see the bluish green booklets in front of me. At the end of every month the postman brought a new booklet, at the end of every month I sent in my written exercises to be corrected. I did my homework so well that I received praise. Only once was there a remark that the exercises had been done rather carelessly. I worked all the more carefully the following weeks.

My passion for diligence, for work, for study. And the desire to be self-educated.

Why of all things did I choose English? In those days English was not as much in demand as it is today, no one would have thought of requiring English to be taught at primary school. Even at the secondary level it was an optional subject, and in Langendorf it was only on offer in the third year. I'd seen the advertisement in the *Volk*, you could send for free information. I liked the idea of learning English all on my own, of doing something special. Not a minute without useful employment. It had to be something new, something completely new, that would activate and satisfy my eagerness to learn.

In my third year at secondary school, just before Christmas, I'd finished working through the last of the green booklets, I'd sent in the final exercises and compositions and had subsequently been notified that I'd completed the course successfully. Sixteen of those green booklets, sixteen months, so I must have started on the course in the summer of my second year at the secondary school.

In that second year the danger that I might be sent back to the village school like my sister Katherine had receded. I was no longer in constant fear of failing a test. Now I could be almost sure of becoming not only a model schoolboy but also a good student. Every week I looked forward to the tests with anxious confidence.

I created a working space for myself in the attic, up front by the window. As there was no light up there, I extended a wire from the socket down in the living room. I made myself a table to go beside the window, and placed a cupboard and a large chest between the chimney and the sloping roof so that I had a room that was closed on three sides. A box spring bed base placed on two lengths of squared timber completed the furnishings. This little room could only be used after April and until October: in the winter it was much too cold, and in July and August you couldn't sleep or work there, directly under the roof tiles, it was too hot. However in the in-between seasons I felt comfortable there, I had something like a room of my own, a hideaway, a den, a haven.

From the kitchen table I can see the mountain. In the early morning I often look that way. Is there a light moving diagonally up the slope through the dawn? At what height are the wafts of mist drifting by? Are the cliffs today light grey, dark grey or almost black after the rain?

Up there on the ridge the solitary firs, tiny, like cutouts against the brightening sky. It's been a long time now since the green of summer faded to autumn hues, and some time too since the autumn hues disappeared too. The mountain with its forest and cliffs looks sombre in the morning dusk.

There was a time I used to climb up there every Sunday morning. At other times we'd build a fire in one of the caves in the ravine, it would be winter, we'd toast slices of bread on sticks over the fire. At other times again I'd footslog through the ravine up to the Nesselboden, the Weissenstein, from there down to the Balmberg and via Balm and Oberrüttenen back home.

I see the mountain in the grey light of dawn, see it while I drink my second cup of coffee in the course of the morning. The quarry, the cliffs of the ravine, the swathes of mist along the slopes, the swathes of cloud floating past above the Hasenmatt and the Balmfluh.

I remember collecting firewood up in the forest and dragging it down the screes. I remember the way I'd load it onto the cart and go down through the village with the heavy cart, the way I'd chop the branches into small pieces, sawing up the thicker ones. How proud I was that by the spring I'd already replenished almost the whole of the back half of the attic with firewood for the following winter.

The happy feeling that I was being useful.

And the work didn't keep me from my studies. School had become the centre of my life. At school I was sheltered from my mother's grumblings, from the quarrelling, from the worry about whether my father would or would not bring home his pay packet on Friday evening. As long as I was at school, all those things were kept at a distance. While I was solving maths problems, writing compositions, reciting a ballad by heart, I was safe.

Life in the woods up there, life at school and the farm life at the Furrers': how long it is since I last thought of it! Never quite forgotten, not that, but it had become remote, it had been remote for years, for decades. And now it's back again, within reach, in the early mornings when I'm sitting in the kitchen drinking coffee.

November, December, gloomy now – and probably always were. But in those cold damp days, the permanent hope that things would change, although I'd have been hard put to say exactly what it was I was looking forward to. The first snowfall? Glorious winter sunshine? A new Karl May book under the Christmas tree? The theatrical evening at the Kreuz, the theatrical afternoons in the hall of the Lanco factory? The Langendorf Friends of Nature Saint Nicholas party, the one-act farce in the small hall of the Traube and my leading role in it?

It might have been that, and yet it wasn't quite that. It was what I was waiting for, and yet I expected something more. That was part of being a model pupil – the immediate environment might be grey and limited yet there was always the prospect of something else. I was learning for myself, but at the same time I wanted to be a model for my younger sister. I started on the English course and suggested Katherine should use the same green booklets to learn English too.

Certainly, I'd enjoyed my life of hard work, diligence and orderliness. And yet at the same time there'd always been this feeling of being boxed in, as if this good life was only half a life.

Small hopes? Great expectations?

Now, with Claudia, during that advent season, both were there.

The new Central Library had been opened in the autumn. I often went there, preferably on Thursday evenings when the library stayed open until nine.

Just by the entrance to the open shelves section there were the newspapers. At home we had the *Volk*, the paper for socialists and trade unionists. Here I could easily read reviews in the *Solothurner Zeitung* of the films that were currently showing. I could also read the reviews in the *Bund* and the *Neue Zürcher Zeitung* of films that would shortly be shown in Solothurn. Here I could find out what the critics thought of the plays that had their premieres in Zurich, Bern and Basel.

Thus I knew long in advance what films I could invite Claudia to, which ones would be most suitable.

The reviews of performances at the municipal theatre, too, were more detailed in the *Solothurner Zeitung* than in the *Volk.*

The vague hope that Claudia might turn up in the newly opened library. It did happen once, and we chatted briefly; but then I missed the chance to leave at the same time as her; I could have walked a little way with her, might even have been able to see her home. That was the only time I saw her there. Claudia had other things to do than spend her spare time in the library reading room.

Bede, on the other hand, came regularly. He was usually to be found there on Thursday evenings and Saturday afternoons, but not by the newspapers. 'Reading the papers is a pure waste of time,' he said. 'Big catastrophes, small catastrophes, whether it's the weather or politics, it's always the same, they never come up with anything else. Yes, you're right, at most they're useful for the film guide. Or if you want to know where to go dancing at the weekend. You can only find things worth reading in books.'

Generally he'd be sitting in the reading room at the second or third table just to the right of the glass door. That was his regular seat.

'Books are wonderful. One book leads you on to the next. Nietzsche led me to Freud, Camus to Sartre and Sartre led me on to Marx. Marx and Marxism, in France lots of clever people argue about it. Here Marx and Marxism are nothing but terms of abuse. You should hear my esteemed father! Okay, after all he's not a philosopher, it's enough if he knows all there is to know about diseased bowels. But librarians should know better. Here they've got two editions of *Das Kapital* in the stacks. But do you think they'd lend me a copy? You should have seen the woman's face! And when I insisted that she give me the Marx she called the boss, really! Nyet, no way, things like that will not be supplied to grammar school kids. As though it was a sex book with indecent pictures inside. May God – if He exists – preserve us from bad books! Our small town in the Cold War: even for the little librarian, observing the utmost vigilance is a categorical imperative. So I ordered the Fischer paperback from the bookshop, and got it of course. It's only a selection, unfortunately, but I'll find a way to get the complete *Das Kapital* and also the *Economic and Philosophic Manuscripts* that Sartre so often refers to. And then I'll come and sit at this table here and read those lewd books in public. Someone has to be the first to set a good example. And when if not now?'

One book was not enough for him, there were always three or four books on his table. He took notes, read with evident seriousness, but he didn't mind being disturbed at his work. We'd go out to the entrance hall, in between the metal card catalogue cabinets where you were allowed to talk. He liked having someone listen to him and I liked listening to him.

'You must read Sartre. By the way, they've got almost all his books here, the plays, the novels, *Being and Nothingness*, the lot. And you won't have any problems: they'll let you have anything by Sartre. For the time being anyway. Simply because they haven't noticed yet that he sees his Existentialism as an ideology and nothing more, and Marxism as the only philosophy that counts today. Or else they think that because he sharply criticises the Marxists he must, as an Existentialist, be a Humanist, a Humanist with a capital H and therefore on their side. Of course, he's been criticising his communist colleagues in France for a long time. There's not much Marx, he says, to be found among those people. Once they've joined the Party they give up thinking for themselves, they just come up again and again with the same sample assortment of sentences. Stereotypes, dogmas, no precise analysis, no lively dialectics. The most disparate conflicts are simply tagged with the same old labels. Class struggle is class struggle, petty bourgeois is petty bourgeois, that's settled once and for all, there's nothing new to be found out about it. However, Sartre wants to find out why a person, or a group of people, behaves or behaved one way and not another in a concrete historical situation, why they felt and acted and thought as they did and not some other way. Actually it should be a pleasure for the cold war warriors here to read something like that. Assuming cold war warriors actually read.'

Those Thursday evenings there in the entrance hall of the new library. Leaning side by side against the metal card catalogue cabinets. Claudia never appeared, but at least her classmate Bede was there. His Master's Voice. Often two were the last to leave the building.

2

Pea Soup and Bacon

Projected onto the back wall of the stage: the picture of a Christmas tree, a splendid fir with lots of decorations hanging from its branches. In capitals: THE STOLEN FIR TREE.

WILLY SCHLATTER: Where did you get that from? You didn't buy it, I hope.

STELLA: What do you think? Bruno found it just outside the wood.

WILLY SCHLATTER: Found it, oh indeed. Fell off the forest warden's trailer, I suppose. Well anyway, it's a fine tree, I'll say that …

Usually Mother bought the little fir tree in Langendorf from the Sieber garden centre, mostly not before the evening of the 24th of December, in the sale so to speak.

Christmas without a Christmas tree wouldn't have been Christmas. And the tree had to be richly decorated. Baubles were part of it, not simple, round, smooth, machine-blown ones, but baubles that were ribbed, with complicated hollows and protuberances, elongated, flattened out, some of them with a niche like the one above the Lady altar in Oberdorf where the Virgin's cloak hangs in folds amidst golden clouds. Birds with copper-coloured beaks and long tail feathers, bobbing up and down on coil-spring legs. Little glass bells, clip-on candle-holders with ball-and-socket joints, glitter garlands. And on top of the tree a finial with three balls tapering off into a slender spire.

All these ornaments came from our grandmother. Wrapped in tissue paper they lay in two large cardboard boxes up in the attic, waiting for the annual display.

Advent and Christmas offered additional opportunities to be a model pupil, and they boosted my attempts to turn my family into a model family.

Once I was at secondary school, I took it upon myself to make sure that we always managed to get a fir tree for free. Once already my father had committed the crime in full public view, marching all the way down from the Bellevue through the village with a stolen fir tree. For the sake of the Ganter family's reputation it was better that someone else take care of the matter.

I see myself walking through the motionless air of a December day towards Hazel Wood. The year before, while I was in grade six, I'd performed my spiritual exercises up there every week: remorse, good resolutions, hope of swift improvement. Since then, I knew the area well enough, and I knew where suitable firs were to be found, all I had to do now was to select one by daylight.

The following night I went up to the reconnoitred spot on the edge of the woods. Silence and darkness all around. I looked around me, took a leap into the undergrowth and dropped down into a crouch. The little Christmas trees stood out clearly enough against the dim brightness out on the field. I unclasped my knife and felt for the slim trunk; soon I was sweating, and my heart was probably pounding too.

Then the little fir tree was in the water tub down in the laundry room – a silver fir, nice and symmetrical.

On Christmas Eve I trimmed it at the bottom until it fitted into the silver-painted wooden stand.

The need for self-delusion! When we were still children we used to write to Baby Jesus, although we knew that the letter was nothing but a wish list for our parents and that hardly any of our wishes would be fulfilled. Knowing that, we used to make little presents for each other and give them to our mother for safekeeping. We'd go to bed immediately after supper, so that two hours later we could wake from sleep to blink in the candlelight. From Heaven Above to Earth I Come, Deep in the Night when Shepherds Awoke, Joseph Dearest Joseph Mine.

Father made fun of it. 'A day like any other, we don't even get off work early.' However he never ever came home late that day, and certainly never stayed away. He was always there, even for supper, sometimes he'd bought some gift or other, and anyhow he was always in a good mood. But that was hardly thanks to the peacemaking influence of the Christian feast day. In all Oberdorf and Langendorf, even in the town, there wouldn't have been a single pub open that might have kept him away from home. It was the lack of pub warmth that drove him home on that evening.

Moreover, in case that was not enough incentive, he was also drawn home by pea soup and bacon. It was something that was never lacking, the robust home-made soup, not simply concocted from Maggi cubes, but cooked in advance to a floury consistency with a big lump of bacon in it.

And now it would be heated up as soon as Christmas Eve was underway. The objects that had been lying in the cardboard boxes for a year now sparkled on the tree; red and white candles filled the room with flickering light; the air was filled with the scent of melting wax, of mandarin and apple peel. Together the children sang the songs they'd learned at school, and then, with a great show of delighted surprise, everyone unwrapped their gifts.

A pause in family warfare. A truce, even if only a precarious one.

After the songs had been sung, the Christmas poems recited, the sparklers lit, the gifts exchanged, it was time for the soup. It was not taken in the kitchen but in the living-room. The table had been spread with a white cloth with ironed folds. Lavish helpings of mustard were squeezed onto the rims of the plates.

The Ganters' Christmas party. Once upon a time. Tell us the stories of old.

At the height of my endeavours to be not only a model pupil but also a model person, this was the most appropriate occasion for me to impart the Biblical worldview to my family. I recited from the Gospel of Matthew and got Rita to accompany the relevant parts by carols on her recorder. I went to great lengths to choose the right gifts, forcing myself to choose not according to my own likings but according to what the recipient would have liked, even if it was completely incompatible with my own tastes. I helped Mother do the baking and generally lent a hand wherever it seemed necessary. For I was a model son and accordingly strove to be the son of a model family.

They let me have my way. But it was no use, there was no lasting success.

Later I confined myself to supplying the tree.

That's what I did again that December.

3

'Requiem for a Nun'

What would I give Claudia for Christmas?

On the two occasions I'd been at the Carrels' place up to then, Bede and Jacob had quarrelled about music, about Beethoven, Bach, Mahler, Elvis Presley and Louis Armstrong, and Claudia had joined in. So I could buy her a record. But wasn't that like ladling water into the Aare with a soup spoon? There were several pianos in the house on the Aare, there was even one in the basement, and the cupboards were full of music scores and gramophone records. Besides that, with her father's Revox Claudia could record every concert that was broadcast on the radio. And anyway I knew nothing at all about those things.

So the only option was a book, for at least I'd talked about books with Claudia on our visits to the cinema. She read a lot and she liked reading: Stifter, Hofmannsthal, Carossa, Bergengruen. She also read Thornton Wilder – I was relieved to know that she also read that American author.

I'd always given books to my two sisters at Christmas. But usually I was the one who devoured those books between Christmas and New Year. Now at last I knew a girl who didn't turn her back on books, someone who loved books. That made it all the more important to choose the right one.

Besides the books I had to read for school, I read mainly American books: plays, novels I'd seen films of, Steinbeck's *The Grapes of Wrath*, *East of Eden*, Hemingway's *For Whom the Bell Tolls*, Melville's *Moby Dick*.

It had started with William Faulkner, his *Requiem for a Nun* at the Schauspielhaus theatre in Zurich. That was during my gap year after secondary school. I'd broken off my office apprenticeship at Autophon after only four weeks and had already been labouring on building sites for Fröhlicher & Co for six months.

Zurich in winter, the Advent season. The new post office building on Schaffhauserplatz, the job high up on the scaffolding, in the cold. At first, the room in a cheap hotel in Schaffhauserstrasse, later the basement room in the big house on Hadlaubsteig. Fröhlicher & Co were not the constructors of the post office building, they'd simply been subcontracted by Bargetzi Stonemasons to mount the limestone panels on the façades. We worked in a team of four: two builders and two labourers; and occasionally Bargetzi sent along a stonemason for a couple of days to help. My main job was to fill the joints between the already fitted panels with mortar, and then clean the limestone until there were no cement streaks left to be seen. The work was monotonous, but I was glad to have been sent to Zurich: at last I could live in a city! And thanks to the expenses I received on top of my wages, and of which I didn't spend more than half, I benefited moneywise too.

I planned to take the entrance examination for the Teachers Training College the following spring. So in the evenings I swotted down in my basement room on Hadlaubsteig. Often, however, I was too tired to revise French verbs, so I went to the cinema.

And once I went to the Schauspielhaus: *Requiem for a Nun* by Faulkner. The following week I went again, and later on I saw the play a third time.

Thanks to the Schauspielhaus, I realised that Solothurn also had a theatre and that there, for a modest price, I could see real dramas, tragedies, comedies. Before that I'd only ever been to plays in the hall of the Kreuz in Oberdorf or in the Lanco hall in Langendorf.

On one of my first visits to the cinema with Claudia – it must have been Laurence Olivier's *Hamlet* film – I'd mentioned those first visits to the Schauspielhaus in Zurich. Claudia had seemed to listen with interest. It was something I could allude to if I gave her a book now. Unfortunately, *Requiem for a Nun* was out of print, but instead of that I could give her *Sanctuary*, the novel that Faulkner had written twenty years before and which contained the backstory of *Requiem*. So I ordered the German translation, together with the American original, at Lüthy's bookshop.

I knew *Sanctuary*. I'd found the Ullstein paperback – small print, cheap paper, and a bare-bosomed woman on the front cover – more than a year earlier in the revolving bookcase here at Lüthy's. I'd immediately bought it, and the same weekend I'd read it from cover to cover in feverish haste. But now that I held the bound book and the Penguin edition in my hands I had misgivings. Was *Sanctuary* the right book for Claudia? Was rape, depravity, vice, lynching, in American English and in German, a suitable Christmas gift? What was I trying to tell Claudia? Did I want to provoke her, like Bede? Or did I only want to give myself airs? All summer long I'd read books Claudia liked, and I myself had liked them too. Should Claudia, by the same token, read the books I liked? And what if she didn't like them?

A few days before Christmas Eve I found a paperback in the bookshop with plays by Eugene O'Neill; *Dramatic Masterpieces* was the title on the cover. That would be just the thing, fascination with America in decorous guise, no one could object to dramatic masterpieces by O'Neill.

It was too late for me to give Claudia the book personally. On the 24th of December I took it to the post office in Langendorf.

Claudia sent me a card, thanking me in bold handwriting without flourishes.

'What exactly made you choose to do English at university?' asks Anna.

'You should start by asking me what made me go to university in the first place. It was Erica's idea, but you know that already. Without Erica I'd hardly have gone to university, I wouldn't have read English or anything else, I'd simply have stayed put as a village schoolmaster. And why not? A village schoolmaster or a grammar school teacher, there's not much difference – although that's something my old colleagues in Olten didn't want to hear. And something even my new colleagues at the teacher training college here were reluctant to admit. And now that the college has become a "university of applied sciences and arts", they'll absolutely refuse to hear any such thing.'

'So you think a teacher's a teacher from the kindergarten to the university, it's basically the same.'

'Only nearly the same, admittedly. Teach all people all things: that would be quite something! But finally I chose to teach only English. What's strange is that I became a teacher, and stayed a teacher, although from early on I'd always preferred to study on my own. Just me and a book, no need for a teacher. I attended as few lectures as possible at university, usually only the ones that had something to do with the paper I was working on at the time. Of course I had good reasons for going to Zurich as seldom as possible: all that time Erica was working as a teacher, while I was in charge of the housework. And then she didn't want to put off having children any longer; but she only took short maternity leaves. So I had paternal duties too, changing nappies, giving the bottle and all that. By the time I had to look after you I was writing my licentiate paper. As it happens, the two things were easy to combine. I've never worked as efficiently since! At all events my studies didn't suffer. And anyway I'd decided right from the start to do no more than the minimum. I wanted to get my degree as quickly as possible.'

'And – were you quick?'

'No, of course not, at least not quick enough. In particular I wasted a lot of time trying to improve my dissertation. And by that time I was already giving your brother the bottle.'

'So that's why I have this feeling that you were always at home. I can remember more about you than about Erica, and more distinctly too.'

'Well I'm sure you don't remember being bottle-fed. But of course I was at home a lot in those days. That's what we'd agreed on. Erica considered that having only one child didn't make sense. Nevertheless, she never thought for a moment of giving up teaching for any length of time for the sake of her children, life as a full-time mother and housewife was out of the question for her. And you know what she's like, if she's made up her mind to do something she does it. And not only for herself, she has no compunctions about meddling in other people's lives. My studies, our marriage, having children, buying the house in Winznau so soon … If she thinks something's a good idea she'll go into action immediately, quick to decide, her decisions firm. Why put something off until tomorrow when you can get started today? Somehow, I liked that. It was something I really liked at the time.'

'Erica the resolute, I know …'

'You're resolute too, and you should be glad that you are.'

It's certainly true, Erica brought movement into my hesitant life.

I can see her sitting in the atrium at the University of Zurich. It's just before Christmas and I've finally got the licentiate exams behind me. 'Do your dissertation while you're at it,' she says. 'Why wait, now that you're in the thick of it? There's no need to look for a job at the moment, there's no hurry. I'll teach, I like teaching, and you can write your dissertation and take care of Anna. And in the holidays I'll take over, so you can dedicate yourself heart and soul to Faulkner.'

Faulkner then, Anderson now.

It's not Erica's fault that it all took much longer than planned. But in the end I did manage to get the dissertation finished, and at exactly the right time too. The Kantonsschule in Olten had just been extended and there were a few new jobs open in the new concrete building up on Hardwald Hill. For a year I was employed as an assistant teacher, then I got a permanent post. How easy such things were in those days! And it will hardly have been due to personal merit. They needed someone who'd majored in English, and simply gave preference to local applicants over strangers.

My move from Olten to the teacher training college in Solothurn followed the same pattern. None of the teachers there at the time had majored in English. They asked me and I accepted. Albeit after considerable hesitation. Change jobs at fifty? Whatever for? No, Erica had no objections. She never had any objections when I ventured upon something new for once.

VIII

ALMOST A LOVE STORY

'This is life's sorrow:
That one can be happy only where two are;
And that our hearts are drawn to stars
Which want us not.'

Edgar Lee Masters, *Spoon River Anthology*

1
What next?

And what came next? What ought to have come next?

I'd got to know Claudia at the rehearsals in Lee Forest, I'd invited her to the cinema a first time, and several times after that, I'd invited her to the theatre a first time, then a second time, I'd bumped into her once at the Central Library. I'd stood in her garden with Bede and his clique to serenade her, had sent her a book at Christmas and she'd thanked me with a card. Now it was January and I didn't know how to go on, I didn't know what came next.

On stage in the Kreuz and in the Langendorf concert hall I'd had to embrace a woman a couple of times in my role as a young suitor. But it was only acting, the script told me what to say, before, after and in beween. Admittedly what I had to say on stage was rather silly. I'd have preferred the kind of things the characters of Tennessee Williams and Eugene O'Neill say in similar situations.

But what was to be done when I wasn't on stage, when I was standing at the Carrels' front door saying good night to Claudia after a visit to the cinema? After a show that had actually offered plenty of examples of the action to be taken at a front door in the middle of the night. I hadn't even put my arm around her shoulder, or made a fleeting attempt to seize hold of her arm, nothing like that, I'd never dared.

My ineptitude was absurd and I was fully aware of its absurdity.

In the Carrels' basement flat Glühwein had come into vogue.

It had begun at the onset of the carnival, in the night from Wednesday to Thursday. Bede and the others had decided to meet at the Carrels' house and to wait there until five in the morning when it would be time for the *Chesslete* parade. The Carrels' house had become the meeting place for such things.

It was Bede who'd brought along the wine. 'There's plenty more of this vinegar where I got it from. Add a bit of sugar and it's sure to be quite *comme il faut.*'

Claudia's sister fetched the ingredients from upstairs. Then, on the electric plate in the utility room where we'd always boiled the water for Nescafé, the brew was prepared. Wine, water, sugar, cinnamon, raisins and dried apple slices, bring to the boil, allow to stand for a short period, bring to the boil again, keeping the pan covered all the while.

People showed the noisemakers they'd brought for the *Chesslete*. Claudia had got hold of a small wooden rattle, her sister had a pair of cymbals, Corinne had a tambourine. Conrad had brought his trumpet; he was quite a good player, something I hadn't known beforehand. Jacob had a primitive kind of xylophone that he could carry by means of a wide band around his neck. Elizabeth had managed to find an old car horn. The cow bell I'd borrowed from the Furrers was also handed around. 'With that you'll bring a touch of peasant carnival to the town,' said Bede. He himself didn't have anything to show. 'On the contrary,' he said. 'This here, the most important thing!' He stretched out a hand holding two earplugs. 'If you give me your xylophone,' he said to Jacob, 'you can have them, your pianist's ears need them more.'

Contrary to convention we drank the mulled wine in little sips; in keeping with convention we drank it in large quantities. 'What a brew,' said Jacob. The next serving was already simmering in the big pot in the utility room.

The *Chesslete* didn't begin until five a.m., we had a long wait ahead.

Elizabeth suggested we listen to music.

'What about something loud with strident brass and booming drums to attune us to the noise? Or else something quiet and smooth because you'd like to have a bit of sleep before we go?' asked Jacob. 'Stravinsky's *Sacré du printemps* for example, that'd be loud enough. Or what about the *Goldberg Variations*? Just the thing for now, not as a soporific of course, which is what the said Herr Goldberg commissioned them for. No, for us they shall be a stimulant. Who's in favour? Who's against? As for me, I'm in favour.'

'Why not?' said Elizabeth. 'But not canned. Only if you play the variations yourself. I know you're practising them, play us a couple. Whether it keeps us awake or sends us to sleep depends entirely on you.'

He had to be pleaded with. But when Claudia's sister brought him the score he sat himself down at the piano and began to play, and he didn't stop. From time to time he lost his place and had to start all over again. But he only laughed and said he was playing Glühwein Variations freely adapted from Goldberg and Bach.

So another hour went by.

'And now? Shall we sing some student songs? Who knows a joke? We've still got ages to go before the noise begins.'

'You should have thought of that before, it was your idea to come here.'

'Yes, unfortunately. It's not the best idea I ever had. How lovely it would be in bed now. But then I'd be bound to miss the *Chesslete*.'

'Come on, let's dance. Blues and jazz.'

Billie Holiday, Louis Armstrong, Miles Davis, the Modern Jazz Quartet. Jacob selected the records – he was au fait with jazz too. With a cigarette hanging out of the corner of his mouth, he regaled us with anecdotes. Most of the time I was the only one listening to him. The others danced.

At first they danced in the corner room, then they opened the door to the veranda over in the extension. It was chilly out there, and the cold streamed in through the door. But that didn't worry anyone: dancing and drinking Glühwein warmed them enough.

Again Bede made fun of the Carrels' house. 'It's like something out of Stifter. That extension there, the first thing you see, coming from town. Is it a garage? Or is it a boathouse? In the back, on the road side, it's clearly a garage; in the front, on the Aare side it's a boathouse, of course; both parts are impressive, two-storied, with a roof terrace out back and, in the front, a pent roof, a boathouse roof, just as I said. But when you're down by the garage door you can hear piano music coming from upstairs, so it's not only a garage and a boathouse but also a music pavilion, a small concert hall, something like that. It's only when viewed from the garden that everything seems clear, the whole of the side wing is a two-storied summerhouse: on the ground floor, the veranda with windows, on the floor above, the open veranda under the pent roof. And when by chance you see sheets hanging there, you conclude that the whole thing is not only a garage plus a concert hall plus a boathouse plus a summer house but a wash house as well. Herr Carrel came up with some good ideas for that extension.'

'A boathouse? If only,' said Claudia's sister. 'But when have you ever seen a boat there? In any case it isn't an extension, we never built any extensions. The house was planned like that from the start. You don't believe me? Shall I show you the plans?'

And what about me, what did I say? Bede talked enough. Jacob talked enough.

'Of course everything was better in the past. It's a simple fact, you don't need to prove it,' mocked Anna.

'Very true! Forget about Albert Schweitzer in Lambarene, Sartre and Camus in Paris, forget them, forget Piaf, Bob Dylan, forget even the Beatles. They don't interest young people any longer. They think DJ Bobo's great!'

'Or Federer.'

'Or Britney Spears.'

'Spears? Where did you get that from?'

'I listen to the radio every day. Federer the tennis ace, the Spears woman, and that Bobo, they're the greatest these days.'

'Maybe. But are you sure that all the young people back then saw your Marlon Brando and your Laurence Olivier as the great stars? Not to mention Camus and Sartre.'

'People knew them, everyone knew them.'

'You expect me to believe that? You don't believe it yourself.'

'Fifty-eight, fifty-nine and the years just after, they were good years, you see. And sixty-eight – that, of course, was the apogee. After that everything went from bad to worse, youth, us, everything.'

'Quite. From bad to worse. Everything. Sure!'

2

The Crooked Tower Bastion

In the summer I'd often gone to the mound of the Crooked Tower. Up there, leaning with my back against the mighty wall, when I looked up river across to the opposite bank I could see the Carrels' house, the longish house with the conspicuous extension of which I didn't know then if it was only the garage or also a boathouse. I'd stand there on the mound, looking across, and the Aare flowed past, broad and quiet; or I'd sit on the bench, do my homework, and occasionally cast a glance across the water to the garden, the house. That was where

Claudia lived, she there, I here, distant, near, only the Aare between us.

The following winter I only seldom came back here. I'd invited Claudia to the cinema; together with Bede, Jacob and the others between the Aare and the house, I'd sung 'In the Black Whale at Ascalon', I'd been taken along, I'd set foot in the house. It had been so simple.

'Come early, at seven if you want. Then we'll have enough time to decide what film we want to see.' It was Claudia's suggestion. It would be the first time we didn't meet in front of the cinema, the first time I went to pick her up at her house.

Punctually at seven I was at the door, and Claudia's sister sent me down to the basement.

Claudia immediately agreed that we'd go and see *The Young Lions*. There wasn't anything else worth seeing. And since we had a lot of time left she turned on the Revox. She lay on the couch, her chin propped up on her hands.

The slowly rotating reels, the birdsong.

Yes, it must have been that evening.

The film was being shown at the Rex. Marlon Brando as the German lieutenant on the campaign in France. Later, he drives through the desert on a heavy motorbike with a captain on his pillion, his face showing his ambivalent inner life. Towards the end of the film, he smashes up his submachine gun against a tree trunk, a wooded slope, winter, beech trunks, he rolls down the slope, bleeding.

Guilt, atonement, involvement, fate, and the way Brando with his dyed blonde hair makes you think of Siegfried in the Nibelungen: there was plenty to talk about as we stepped out into the cold. We crossed Dornacherplatz, sauntered through the Vorstadt quarter, Claudia didn't seem to be in a hurry. Brando as the average German who only gets to know little by little what the *Wehrmacht* is forcing him to do. You see how averse he is to harassing the French in occupied Paris. How, after a battle in the desert, he balks at shooting wounded soldiers. And how, much later, during the retreat in France, happening to land up in a concentration camp that's just been vacated, he has to listen to an officer grumbling that they hadn't had enough staff.

Prisongasse, Unterer Winkel, Oberer Winkel. Did Claudia lead us in the direction of the Bastion or did I? It can hardly have been by chance that we finally found ourselves standing at the foot of the mighty wall. We climbed up the ramp, went to the front, looked across over the railway bridge and the Aare to dimly lit Postplatz. A goods train approached from West Railway Station, thundered towards us across the bridge.

Over on the opposite bank, the building of the agricultural cooperative, the post office, the house façades on Landhausquai, all in dim stage lighting; while here, in the dark, a premiere was starting, without a dress rehearsal or indeed any rehearsal at all. Heads bumped, teeth grated on teeth; until Claudia, bending her head to one side, took over. Kisses don't taste sweet, only strange, of saliva. Mind the front teeth!

It was like being in a silent movie. Some time or other we'd have to talk again, but that wasn't urgent at the moment.

'Can you see our house from here?' Claudia asked.

'Probably,' I said and led her along the wall to the other side of the tower.

Midnight, frosty early March. Fumbling hands between coat and sweater.

After I'd accompanied Claudia down from the mound and past the Altes Spital, across the bridge and along the Aare road back to her home, and I was standing alone again beneath the railway bridge, it suddenly occurred to me: she's been going out with her friends for a long time, with Bede, with Jacob, with Conrad, or with somebody else I don't even know, she doesn't only know these things from films, she lives in town, she's had more practice in these things than I have, and anyway nothing works the first time, it's all hard work, you have to keep on trying, again and again.

I looked across the Aare, across to the mighty wall surrounding the mound.

So that's what it was like. I took my left hand out of my coat pocket, brushed my half-open mouth over the back of it, over the ball of my thumb, carefully pressed my teeth into the flesh, nipped each of my finger tips, one after the other, with my lips. What does that feel like? What effect does it have on the girl it's being done to? My clammy fingers didn't yield much in the way of experience.

In the trilogy there's a bench with a street lamp beside it and a big rising moon in the sky behind. During a long embrace the young man talks to the audience over the girl's shoulder, and then – after a one hundred-and-eighty-degree turn – the girl talks to the audience over the shoulder of the boy. In neither of the monologues is there any talk of love.

'… Push wheelbarrows, mix mortar, point a façade on Schaffhauserplatz, swell with pride, proud heart, those are things I can do, and I've done them long enough. And now, get away from here, a different life at last, far from the Mittelland, out of the fog, up to the Alps, there's sure to be some dam that needs building up there in the high mountains! Off to the remotest mountain valley, the higher the better, the remoter the better, it can't be high enough, remote enough. Up there for a summer, for a winter, the master of giant cement mixers, a helmet on my head, I study plans, go over the calculations again, go over everything once more. The evenings in the shack are long; while the others play cards and drink beer I drink beer and read Brecht, Becket, O'Neill, and my every free moment is spent learning Italian so as to be able to converse with the labourers, steel fixers and crane operators from the Po Valley …'

And more of the kind; with 'to be spoken with passion' in brackets at the beginning.

In her monologue the girl talks about a Red Cross stint in Africa, work in a children's hospital, a vaccination campaign against polio.

At the same time keywords and sentences are projected onto the rear wall of the stage under the big moon: 'After the Film' – 'Life Plans' – 'Our Town is Small and Neat' – 'What a Wide, Wide World!' …

It was a long time before I told anyone about this premiere on the mound of the Crooked Tower. I wouldn't have dreamed of mentioning it to a male friend, I only ever related the story to girlfriends. I gave them an account of the surrounding circumstances, of the before and the after too, if I thought such confessions might pay off; I omitted some things, added others, often coming quite close to what had really happened. The fact that I was already nineteen by the time I took my first kissing-course had already been confidence-inspiring for Verena from Matzendorf, and much later on had had an extraordinarily stimulating effect on Monica from the Zurich Oberland. And as to Lena, the bookseller in Solothurn, who had totally forgotten the corresponding episode in her own biography, since things like that had only ever happened en passant and as if they were the most natural thing in the world – surprisingly, my Crooked Tower story made her sad. In the Ganter family shows of tenderness had been rare, I certainly can't recall any hugs or kisses. A handshake was all that could be expected on arrival or departure.

'What a wide, wide world!' Did I, in that winter of nineteen fifty-eight, pay any attention to what was happening out in the wide world? I listened to the news on the radio, skimmed through the *Volk*, occasionally I also looked at other newspapers in the library reading room, de Gaulle in Algeria, Castro in Havana, the Berlin Ultimatum, Khrushchev and Eisenhower and Mao. I heard about those things, read about them; but even if the big stories out there had had some direct effect on my life, I'd probably hardly have noticed, busy as I was with my own little story.

Yet down in the Carrels' basement there'd often enough been talk about History with a capital H. Communism, capitalism, the Cold War. 'Whoever sows bombs will harvest mushrooms': Bede's words. The Swiss army too had plans to procure atomic weapons. It was only logical: atomic weapons, yes; women's suffrage, no. 'We need the weapons soon, you see; but as to voting rights for women, we Swiss can do without them for a long time yet, whatever Sartre and Simone de Beauvoir may say.'

And what's going on right now far away in the world? Do I pay more attention than I did then? Atom bombs are still around, even if they hardly get a mention any more, they only make the headlines when North Korea boasts that they've got the bomb too now, or when the Americans maintain that the mullahs in Iran are about to have it.

Everyone says the Cold War is over. Is it? Whatever the case, a replacement has been found long since: democracy versus terrorism and rogue states.

All quiet in the Near East.

And what about the Far East? The surge of China. Benno, my daughter's boyfriend, likes telling stories about the Chinese dragon. A strange mixture of communism and capitalism. Whatever's useful from the one, and from the other? Benno has his doubts.

And on top of the political evils, every month the big natural catastrophe. At the turn of the year it was the tsunami in the Indian Ocean. Next it'll be an earthquake or a typhoon or a flooding in North Germany.

Swiss Radio DRS, Deutschlandfunk, the BBC, news, reports from news correspondents, everything brought to me at my kitchen table at six in the morning. What shall I do with it all? Has it got anything to do with me? Should I send the Red Cross or Swiss Solidarity a few hundred francs? Sign a petition on the internet? Refuse to buy oranges from Israel? But what about the oranges from Spain that have been picked by poorly paid North Africans?

3

Glühwein helps

Two or three weeks had gone by since, leaning with my back against the wall of the Crooked Tower mound, I'd coped rather unsatisfactorily with my own and somebody else's lips. Afterwards I'd practised on the heel of my hand and on my fingertips, but the last part of our way along the Aare still filled me with apprehension. Halfway through March, Claudia was as capricious as April weather. If she'd arranged to meet me at eight in front of the Elite cinema, she didn't arrive until half past. And if, below the flickering screen, she then gave my arm a quick squeeze to apologise for having made us miss the beginning of the film, in the intermission she soon fell into a sullen silence, and then tortured me with her taciturnity on the way home through the dark Obach quarter. If, to be on the safe side, I already asked midweek if I could take her to the theatre the following Saturday, she accepted warmly, but the next day, in the long break, she came by to say that, unfortunately, she wasn't free on Saturday after all. My only consolation was that she'd gone to the trouble to look for me during the break so that she could tell me.

And now, at least, when we went out together I always picked her up at the house on the Aare. That seemed to me to be a step forward.

Once, her father came to answer the doorbell. However, I never met her mother.

That evening, too, Claudia had been withdrawn at first, almost hostile. It wasn't a Monday or Tuesday evening at the Elite, or a Saturday evening at the theatre. We'd been to a lecture at the Töpfer Society, the last lecture that winter.

Those lectures were popular among Kantonsschule students, attending them was something young people did in their free time, just as they go to disco parties and concerts at the Kofmehl Club today. That evening, a locally well-known doctor was to give a talk on psychosomatic aspects of gastrointestinal diseases. Claudia went because she wanted to study medicine later on. Since it was a lecture with slides, it wasn't held in the council chambers as usual, but had been relocated to the hall of the vocational school.

The hall was full, the whole Bede clique was there too, and afterwards we all went over to the Carrels' house. Once again, Bede quoted Nietzsche, cited Freud who'd discovered the relationships between the soul and the digestive tract decades ago. It was quite remarkable that psychoanalysis, dreadful psychoanalysis – or at least its medical offshoot – had finally arrived in Solothurn, and that it had been honoured with a big turnout of local people. By the way, said Bede, he knew from his father that the speaker had worked on his lecture for months, and that from the very start he'd been fully aware of the importance of the occasion. A capable man in his field, his father thought a lot of him, he was a colleague he enjoyed arguing with.

No, this time it wasn't the leisurely rotation of the reels on the tape recorder, or the birdsong that Herr Carrel had recorded out in the garden in the summer. This time it was the babel of voices in the house, so often to be heard here till long after midnight, the buzz of voices, dense one moment, scattered the next. Freud, Marx, Sartre, Camus, the Töpfer Society, medical anecdotes, short, middle, and long-term plans for the future, and various outlines of worldviews, and who had seen what film last week – and of course Bede making fun of the teachers as only he could: the way one of them used to stretch his braces out far in front of him while explaining difficult things, then let them smack back onto his plump chest to underline his point. Nail that in your head! With your sine and cosine you'd do better getting a job as a mechanic in the railways!

People were already preparing to leave when someone expressed a wish to hear Mahler.

Jacob picked out the record. While conducting to the music, he commented on it for the benefit of those still sitting there. 'Here he's citing a *Ländler*, and now, listen, that folksong mush, it's all ironic of course.'

Claudia began to tidy up. I helped her wash up the glasses and cups in the utility room. A few isolated sentences amid the loud music that resounded from the main room. I'd never been alone with Claudia back here before, standing beside her at the metal sink.

Out in the room they put on a new record. 'Mahler again,' said Claudia. '*Das Lied von der Erde*, said to be Chinese poems. I don't know why Jacob likes it.'

When we returned to the room with the rest of the Glühwein, he and Corinne and Conrad had already gone. They'd all gone. Claudia's sister wasn't there any more either.

Why had I missed leaving with Jacob? I was embarrassed to be the last.

'Let's listen to this to the end,' said Claudia and poured us Glühwein. As she settled down cross-legged on the sofa I was overcome with stagefright. The contralto voice resounded dark and sad through the empty room.

With silent determination I stood up and went over to the sofa. Silent yes, but determined too? Wasn't it more like panic that made me get up and go across to Claudia? There she was, sitting cross-legged, her head slightly to one side, eyes closed, entirely engrossed in the music.

Forehead to forehead, I in a squat in front of her, then we stood up and staggered along the corridor to the open door of her room.

It was certainly nothing like the wild scene between Brando and Eva Marie Saint in *On the Waterfront*, and it wasn't the kiss between James Dean and Julia Harris on the Ferris wheel, it wasn't Paul Newman or Elizabeth Taylor, no cat on a hot tin roof.

It must have been the Glühwein that got us out of our pullovers. Not the slow spinning of the tape recorder reels – it was the whole room that was spinning now, the armchair, the bookcase, the table, everything was spinning around me, spinning around both of us. Meanwhile, outside, the contralto voice rose, fervent and raw, higher and higher above the hovering strings.

The small pale breasts. That's how far it went. The Glühwein didn't get us any farther. 'No, no, please don't.' She said it straightforwardly, decisively.

Going on would have been going too far.

However, an hour later, as I pushed my bike up the avenue to Langendorf, I started having doubts. That rust-coloured bedspread, the orchestral bursts, and the way Claudia bolted the door. There was something not quite right about it.

4

A Bungled Exit

In the spring holidays I worked as a labourer on a building site: a block of flats in Bellach. I pushed loaded wheelbarrows, pulled empty ones, shovelled gravel into the cement mixer, hauled bricks, dug ditches – hardly jobs that keep your mind busy.

It was something else that kept my mind busy: the premieres with Claudia. Had I done the right thing?

Had I passed the test? And what should I do, what not do, when we resumed?

And besides that, there was a tiny detail. But a tiny newspaper ad that I'd often noticed helped me out of my predicament. I should have attended to the matter much sooner. At least it was something that could be sorted out in advance. The post brought the offer of a wide selection. Discrete delivery guaranteed. Payment was simple: I could pay in postage stamps. And three days later the little parcel had already arrived. Together with the card for further orders they'd also enclosed a leaflet with instructions for use.

The rubber felt like rubber, which inspired confidence. But in my den up in the attic there was nothing I could use to roll the thing over. Eyes open, eyes closed, it was no good, I couldn't get a Claudia to show up for practice.

She didn't appear anywhere else either.

We'd agreed to meet on Saturday morning at the market. I was there by ten o'clock. I pushed through the shoppers, and went on across the Aare to the Vorstadt quarter and up to the mound of the Crooked Tower. Swallows darted around high above the roofs. Leaning against the wall I looked across to the railway bridge and over to Postplatz. The sky was blue. Spring had come. Soon it would be summer, a summer like no other.

Had I stayed too long on the mound? Claudia was nowhere to be found, not in the market square nor in Lüthy's bookshop, nor in front of Nordmann's department store. Up in the bell tower the king and his retinue had already came out of the little door, had moved in a semicircle to the other side and disappeared, traders had already started to clear away their stalls. We'd arranged to meet at eleven, I waited until twelve thirty.

When I phoned her at the Carrels' in the afternoon, Barbara answered. She told me that Claudia had gone to town, she hadn't said where exactly or when she'd be back.

Back to Amthausplatz, to the bookshop, Gurzelngasse, Hauptgasse, Stalden, Friedhofplatz. Near the fountain in front of Nordmann's I saw Conrad. We chatted about the holidays and the end of the holidays. He hadn't yet managed to find a girl he could take to the Dornachia fraternity May Ball in Bad Attisholz. He took it for certain that Claudia would be going to the ball too, and that she'd be going with me. The fact that he took that for certain, and that presumably others thought the same, alleviated my doubts.

Late in the afternoon I rang Claudia again from the Furrers' place. Yes, she'd been in town. Yes, unfortunately we'd missed each other. I asked her what she was doing in the evening and suggested going to the cinema. She seemed to hesitate, but then she agreed.

During the intermission between the newsreel and the film we remained mainly silent. I didn't tell her that I'd looked for her all over the market. Nor did I tell her that I'd gone to town again in the afternoon. She nodded to people I didn't know. When our knees bumped into each other by accident she drew hers away. She found the film boring, and when I rose in its defence, she said she didn't want to spoil my pleasure.

I was relieved when I saw that there was something on in the basement of the Carrels' house. Perhaps, with other people there, Claudia's bad mood would disappear.

It was Barbara's party. Some of her old schoolfriends and a couple of people she'd got to know at the university; they were sitting or standing around in the large corner room, dancing in the veranda of the extension.

Soon an architecture student took charge of disgruntled Claudia. Her mood improved – if at my expense. The two of them danced together several times, holding each other closely, too, whenever the music was slow, she sleepy and withdrawn, he smiling over her pageboy haircut. And when they moved apart again, the free and easy way they danced was not quite the thing to reassure me either.

Then Barbara stepped in. She took the future architect away from her sister for the next dance. He couldn't refuse. And very soon she'd totally assumed Claudia's role, and she'd also ensured that the music stayed nice and slow for a long time so that the man was now kept thoroughly busy with her, Barbara. And whilst he continued to wear a smug smile, she looked brightly around the room – something he couldn't see since she had her chin on his shoulder. And at an opportune moment she winked at me, who was now dancing with Claudia, as if to say: I pinched him from her, for your sake.

Ah Barbara, it didn't help much.

Did I sleep with Claudia? Nonsense, of course not! Necking and groping on the Crooked Tower mound, and groping and necking on the Aare embankment under the railway bridge; and once and once only, at

188

the Carrels', the tussle on the rust-coloured, patterned bedspread. And all those pre-rehearsals, rehearsals, dress rehearsals and near-premieres hadn't brought me any closer to Claudia. On the contrary, I'd never before known Claudia to be as changeable in her mood towards me as she was now.

That seemed to suggest that I'd done something wrong. Was she ashamed of what had happened? Had I gone too far? Or hadn't I gone far enough? 'No, please don't' is what she'd said, and for me that was a command. Was it all just too gross for Claudia? Or had the whole procedure simply been laughable, doltish.

So many questions and never an opportunity to talk to her about it. And even if I'd found an opportunity, I'd have been a chump once more and all the more. Was it a good idea, was it even possible to talk about such things? Perhaps it would be even more embarrassing to talk than to hold my tongue.

Missing the moment to leave with Jacob. The sofa scene, the scene in the room and the fact that Claudia so clearly knew more about those things than I did, even though she read books by Adalbert Stifter and Hugo von Hofmannsthal instead of those by Miller, Faulkner and Williams. Did I think I could challenge her superior experience – and I had a feeling it was superior – by aping Marlon Brando? I hadn't gone too far, I hadn't gone far enough, I was a moron and I'd behaved like a moron.

And I continued to behave like a moron. I still persisted in inviting Claudia out. She hardly ever had time, she had all kinds of reasons that sounded increasingly like excuses. She couldn't manage this week, but perhaps next week. She had visitors from the French-speaking part of the country, she had to look after them.

Once I saw her at the Rex with Jacob, after I'd invited her two days before to see the same film. When I came up to them, she seemed more annoyed than embarrassed.

I still went to the Carrels' place, but only in the company of the others.

On one of those Saturday evenings I stole away early, but returned around midnight. The light was still on in the basement and I could easily have gone in again, no one would have thought anything of it.

A spectator at a shadow play. A relapse or a rerun? Attracted, repelled, here I was again, outside the door like last summer. I dodged away from the fence when headlights up on the road beamed through the darkness, when a car door slammed. I stood at the fence, smelled the wild garlic, heard the splash of waves against the riverbank.

And suddenly I found myself standing in the water. Wading, I groped my way along the fence to the garden. Then, dripping wet, plunged deeper into the bushes as voices became audible from over by the house: Barbara or Claudia or someone else, I couldn't make it out. Soft calls, the crunch of footsteps on gravel, the sound of voices, moving off townwards.

Climbing up ash trees, clambering around in elder and willow thickets was something I'd had plenty of practice in from an early age. Now I was sitting in the fork of an ash tree, seeing without being seen, prepared for God knows what discovery.

Again two people came out, walked along the gravel path through the garden, turned off round the corner of the extension, and a couple of seconds later I heard the gate up by the road slam shut. Perched in a tree fork on a balmy May night. What did I hope to see? What did I fear I might see? I realised what an idiotic situation I was in, and how embarrassing it could become. I couldn't think of any civilised reason for being up on the ash tree. Whatever happened I mustn't be caught. As soon as the chase began I'd have to drop down from the tree like a monkey and escape around the fence.

I waited half an hour after all the lights had gone out before I slid down from my perch in the tree. I didn't dare cross the garden, I waded back through the water.

If you want something for long enough you get it in the end. Spare no effort and it can be made to happen. That was the principle that guided my life. And on the same principle I hoped to win Claudia, her respect, her friendship, her confidence, whatever: all the things that were to be found in the books I read, or that were shown so strikingly in the films I saw. If Claudia was always in my thoughts, it was inconceivable that I shouldn't also be in hers. All you had to do was hang on to your passion, and in the end your passion would be reciprocated!

I confused winning someone's love with scrupulously doing one's homework. I thought the strength of a sentiment guaranteed that it would be reciprocated, I thought that when it came to sentiment, too, everything was determined by merit.

Ludicrous! It might be possible to earn the odd act of kindness because a faint feeling of justice is aroused, so that what was given comes back. But twenty acts of kindness still don't make a friendship, they can't be exchanged for love. Love accounts don't balance.

'The pangs of desprized love ...' I should have known, I'd parodied Hamlet's soliloquy often enough. And anyway, wasn't being crossed in love the rule rather than the exception? It had been childish to imagine that an exception would be made in my case.

Later, it would be others who'd be made to suffer. It's never the right people who are hit.

IX

THAT SUMMER – GOING
THROUGH WITH IT

'… I know defeat. I can accept defeat …'

Sherwood Anderson, *Out of Nowhere into Nothing*

1
'The beginning of what?'

I did have a talk with Claudia in the end, in the bicycle park down in the basement of the Kantonsschule.

BRUNO: I don't want to bother you. I understand that you don't want to have anything to do with me any more. It took a long time, but I understand now, I won't bother you any more. You must have noticed that I think a lot of you and that I like you. You must have seen that it was the beginning of something.'

MARGARITA: The beginning of what?

BRUNO: *He gazes at Margarita, stiffens as if winded; his arms drop, he lowers his head and turns away without a word. Exit right. Surprised, the girl remains standing in the front of the proscenium …*

That's the scene as it appeared in the trilogy, just before the end of the second part.

It's followed by three soliloquies, each one introduced by the director, three variations on the 'The beginning of what?' scene.

'… You behaved towards me the way you behave towards everyone else. Always polite, always friendly, you get on well with everyone, your schoolmates, your girlfriends, all your friends, close or distant. No, you don't favour anyone in particular. So why should you favour me, of all people, over all the others? And yet I thought that the friendliness you showed me was a bit more than just friendliness, not much more, just a bit, a tiny bit more, but that was enough for me. Admittedly I couldn't have said exactly what I was hoping for, what exactly I was expecting. However, I see now that I must apologise for having had even the slightest expectations. It was uncalled-for, it was vain, it was stupid. You must find it embarrassing, it must have been embarrassing all along. Well, it's a good thing that it's over now, that it's come out into the open, that it's been cleared up. Yes, it's clear to me now. It should have been clear to me from the start. We don't match, even the blind can see that. But I wasn't only blind, I was also deaf …'

'The beginning of what? That's the question. And if it's you who's asking, it has to be my question too. And here's my frank answer: for me it was not only the beginning of something, it changed absolutely everything. That's something you know, something you must have known for a long time. And what about you? Were those little signs of affection really only superficial, a lovely smooth surface with nothing behind, nothing underneath. Oh no, something did happen, even though it mightn't have been what I thought it was. I can't have been completely mistaken. And you can't have deliberately wanted to fool me, you wouldn't do that. You're not a hypocrite, you can't be …'

'By asking like that you've already given me the answer. It was the beginning of nothing. It was all nothing, nothing at all. It's nice to hear that, high time I heard it. It was all play-acting, and you acted your role splendidly, a brilliant performance. Congratulations, even if it was a play in which I seem to have been the buffoon, the country bumpkin, the yokel. So he hoped something was starting, he believed something had already started. He was mistaken, as is to be expected of a yokel and a buffoon. Which means I performed my role, the yokel role, properly. My only mistake was that I took the role too seriously. *Tant pis, tant mieux*, serves the buffoon right.'

What did I really say down there in the basement of the Kantonsschule? I'd spent a long time preparing myself for this conversation, then everything happened very fast. I'd hardly started when it was already over.

Weeks after our meeting, new versions of what I should have said kept going through my head. A poor exit, that's what it had been. No clarification, no catharsis, no melancholic funeral oration for my first and only love. Before that I'd already done several things I was ashamed of. With this performance I'd made everything even worse. No, it couldn't end like that. The last word had yet to be said.

And had the question 'The beginning of what?' ever been asked? Did Claudia really ask me something like that? It's there in the next to last scene of part two, I wrote it down, and it's the starting point for the three soliloquies that follow.

No, I don't remember what I said myself. But I do remember that sentence of Claudia's, I remember it with astonishing clarity. I see her face down there in the bicycle park of the Kantonsschule, her stern face, her mouth, her eyes, her forehead, her pageboy hair. Her face shows incomprehension. Or is it embarrassment? Or consternation? And if she did ask that question – and I remember very clearly that she did – then I must have said something beforehand that prompted her to do so.

It had to be set straight. One of the many pitiful mistakes I had to rectify.

But again, what an odd way to rectify it! In one of the soliloquies Margarita's friendliness is branded as pure superficiality, in another the girl is derided for having performed her role brilliantly. Three variations but a single rant, three times without a good exit, three distinct kinds of embarrassment.

'… I've said things to you that I had to say – forgive me – things I had to say in sheer desperation, but that I regretted even as I said them. I felt awful about it. I knew it wasn't right of me to say those things, but I had to, and it made me feel awful …'

Or did I simply want to show that the hero is always too late with his answers? Did I want to show how a single sentence can continue to have an effect for many weeks? Was it the discrepancy between what the hero thinks and what he actually says. Or – since for once I had enough ideas for this scene – did I simply churn out lines in order to stretch out the second part of the trilogy to a decent length?

2
'The moon over the allotments'

At first it was only the decision to go to Zurich. The conversation with Claudia had taken place on a Monday. Two days later it became evident that I couldn't stand it here any longer, that I had to get away: even the longest walk through Hazel Wood, or the long Wednesday afternoon slog up the Weissenstein and then over to the Hasenmatt couldn't take me far enough away.

Should I flee to France? To Paris to the Existentialists? It had to be something extraordinary, unprecedented. If nothing had begun, at least the end should be spectacular. Not that unfortunate meeting down in the bicycle basement, not that idiotic flight after I'd been left speechless.

For Whom the Bell Tolls. Gary Cooper behind the machine gun: that would have been a dignified exit, off and away, freedom and the fight for the good cause in the Spanish Civil War. And now, the Foreign Legion as its contemporary counterpart? No, that would be going too far. Besides, I knew of no film that could have served as a model. Therefore France with Paris was out of the question.

Zurich was nearer. It was also a big city that might offer big city adventures. Especially if I tried to hitch a ride there. Early on Ascension Thursday morning I told my mother I had to go to Zurich.

I'd never done hitch-hiking before.

The first car took me as far as Schönenwerd. Here the waiting began. What with repeated waitings I didn't arrive in Zurich until the middle of the afternoon. As I stood on the edge of the road with my thumb outstretched, all those little disappointments when cars passed by without stopping had for a while taken my mind off the big debacle. By the time I finally found myself in the centre of Zurich, I already felt almost relieved and thankful.

I walked to the main station, bought a bar of chocolate at the kiosk and ate it with the rest of the bread I'd taken with me as provisions. Then I put my backpack and my raincoat in a locker and went through the Niederdorf towards the lake. I spent the late afternoon sitting in the sun on the Limmat river quay and beside the lake.

In the early evening I went up to the Schauspielhaus theatre.

Thornton Wilder's *The Skin of Our Teeth* was on. I sat right in the back in one of the cheap seats. Surprisingly, the mix and muddle of Ice Age and Stone Age, Noah's Flood and bomb warfare cheered me up. In one and the same scene, a baby dinosaur and a mammoth as pets, together with Moses, Homer and a telegraph boy! Even in the face of disaster Mr Antrobus invents the wheel, the alphabet and the multiplication table; and, notwithstanding all the adversities, Mrs Antrobus keeps her family together, no easy job with Cain as a son and Lilith as a nanny.

Nothing in the world is more normal than getting into a catastrophe, and part of it, too, is that you always manage to escape. Slapstick or not, if Thornton Wilder said it, there must be something to it, and I had the whole night ahead to think about it.

I didn't dare go and sleep on a bench in the middle of town. Out in the suburbs, I'd be more likely to find somewhere to lie down. During my gap year, when I'd helped put up the façade of the new post office building on Schaffhauserplatz, I'd lived for a couple of weeks in the basement of a house on Hadlaubsteig. As far as I remembered, not very far above that steep road the houses ended and the woods began. Back then had been the first time I'd gone to the Schauspielhaus, Faulkner's *Requiem for a Nun*; and later I'd thought of giving the backstory of that play to Claudia for Christmas, but then I'd replaced it at the last moment with a book of plays by Eugene O'Neill; and now again I'd seen a play by an American: all that could hardly be coincidence.

I vaguely knew the direction, first along the tramlines and then to the right, uphill. Whenever a turning seemed familiar I took it; if a street seemed unfamiliar I turned back. After losing my way several times I found myself at the foot of Hadlaubsteig after all. By which time it must have been almost midnight. If I continued in a zigzag up the hill I'd reach the edge of the town and the woods.

I saw that there was a path leading off from the tarmac road through the trees. I took a few steps into the dark, further on it grew lighter again. Then I was standing in front of an iron gate. Out there in the open I could see the vegetable patches, the bushes, the roofs of sheds – here I was sure to find a place to sleep.

I chose a shed with a porch. Hours and hours by the roadside, hours loitering alongside the Limmat river and the lake, the walk here: exhausted I sat down on the bench. Leaning my back against the wall I looked out across the little roofs, the bushes, the vegetable patches, on my right the edge of the wood, over there the row of street lamps, most likely the boundary of the allotments. Far below, the lights of the city.

I began to feel cold. In a corner of the porch among all kinds of implements I found a straw mat and a piece of sacking. The bench was too narrow and too short, I lay down on the wooden floor on top of the mat and covered myself with my jacket and the sacking. I'd left my raincoat in the locker, I could really have done with it now. Rustlings in the woods, gusts of wind in the bushes nearby. From the theatre to the garden hut, my situation was ridiculous, lying on the ground was ridiculously uncomfortable, luckily nobody knew.

All of a sudden I started up.

This allotment here will be in it; my night climb up here and the sunlit steps of the Limmat river quay this afternoon, my crazy flight from Oberdorf to Zurich Niederdorf, they'll all be in it. What's just happened and what happened before that, what might have happened, and what will or might happen in the future. The escape by the skin of my teeth in the Schauspielhaus now, and for years Williams, O'Neill, Miller et cetera, and that I'd seen Faulker's *Requiem*, his only play, that winter. And the rehearsals in Lee Forest a year ago, and father's village theatricals all the years before and my own roles in them, the whole to-do right from the beginning. And late summer, autumn, great expectations and the mulled wine and the pain and the embarrassment. Making the best of a bad job? Of course not, exit, swansong, requiem for a model schoolboy, that's what it all added up to.

Why hadn't it occurred to me a long time ago?

The way out.

There was no question of sleep any more. The hut roofs in the moonlight, the flowerbeds and bushes and rain barrels and little paths in the moonlight. And the smell of flowering plants, of grass, of leaves. I sat there quietly, wide awake.

Before the sun rose I was already on my way down to the town. Hadlaubsteig and the house on Hadlaubsteig and the street lamp down on the corner and the crossing will all be in it, and the route I took back then, straight through the residential area to Schaffhauserplatz, the post office building with its façade of shell limestone from Estavayer, and how I'd pointed the joints high up on the scaffolding, and the site hut where I used to eat my bread and my caraway sausage at lunchtime: everything will be in it. What a farce, hitch-hiking to Zurich! But now the Gordian knot had been cut, the decision taken.

I washed my face and my arms in the station toilet. Then I went up to the Lindenhof park, sat down in the morning sun and waited for the shops to open. I bought milk and rolls in a Migros shop and went back to my bench in the Lindenhof park.

I'd stay in Zurich for today.

It was my first time skipping classes.

I bought a notebook and a ballpoint pen at the Sankt Annahof store. I had to make an immediate note of all the things that occurred to me for the play. And in the evening I'd go back to the Schauspielhaus.

I had a whole day ahead of me.

I didn't go to the Schauspielhaus again that evening after all. I was aware all over my body that I hadn't washed for two days, I'd only been able to wet my face and arms occasionally. I didn't feel comfortable about sitting in the theatre smelling of sweat. The cinema was another matter, I could choose a seat where there'd be no one sitting right next to me.

I've forgotten the name of the cinema. What about the film? Something grim about the American South, I don't remember the director or the actors either. I suppose that from time to time I dozed off in the comfortable seat. But I do remember that after the performance I went to Stauffacherplatz. Then back to Bahnhofstrasse, Bellevue, past the Opera House to the outskirts, along the lake wherever possible.

I didn't get outside the residential area this time, there were no allotments on the way to Küsnacht. After a long walk I turned back. In the Zürichhorn park I sat down on a bench and waited for sunrise, and finally, as the sun started to warm the air, I managed to get a bit of sleep.

It was high time to return home. The exercise book with its stiff cover was half filled with notes, that was a good start, now I had to get down to work. This time I wouldn't hitchhike, I had no time for trivial adventures, I had other things to do.

On my way through the Niederdorf to the station I rummaged in a box of books outside a second-hand bookshop. I can't remember what I was looking for, but the book I found is still in the bookcase in Winznau: Edgar Lee Masters, *Spoon River Anthology*. Probably I was drawn to the book by its title. On the platform I began to read the poems, on the train I didn't stop reading, and I continued to read while changing trains and waiting in Olten. I'd half-finished the book by the time I arrived in Solothurn. Poems. The dead in a small American town hold monologues from their graves, living autobiographies from the grave. I read on and on, I couldn't get enough.

When I arrived home shortly after midday, my mother showered me with reproaches. It was bad enough having one member of the family roving around for days without our having any idea of his whereabouts. Was I starting on that now? And anyway, shouldn't I have been at college yesterday and today? She certainly would not sign an excuse, she'd have nothing to do with it.

I defended myself good-humouredly. She needn't worry, her worries were unfounded. Many of my classmates had already skipped classes, it was something that occurred before difficult tests, not to avoid doing the test but on the contrary to prepare properly for the test. In any case, I hadn't missed much this Friday and Saturday. I'd gone to Zurich to see Thornton Wilder's famous play. Wilder was important, I'd absolutely had to see the play.

I see myself on that Saturday afternoon sitting at the trestle table up in the attic. I kept on writing till late into the night. The first step is the easiest, making plans is easy. I made rapid progress, for I already knew:

the location of the story in the third part of the trilogy would be Zurich, the flat steps of Limmat river quay, the zigzag path up Zurich hill, the allotments, the bench on Lindenhofplatz, various benches by the lake, plus a few scenes in the Niederdorf. I'd already staged it all for myself, so that was settled: the flight to Zurich would be the theme of the third part of the trilogy. A flight, or a penitential journey, or a pilgrimage? In any event, up and away, leaving everything behind, and then finally, after several low points which could be turned into dramatic highlights, the return home. No happy end, and yet courageous, with slogans for a new day: 'Summer is coming! Awake, Christian soldier!'

'How are you getting along with your Anderson?' Anna asked yesterday.

'Slowly, unsteadily. One thing's sure: it's giving me a lot of trouble and it tires me out. Sometimes I'm already back on my bed by the middle of the morning.'

'Not surprising, if you never go to bed before midnight and get up at five.'

'Perhaps. But I'm sure my tiredness also has something to do with my doubts about the point of my work. Life in a small American town, a long, long time ago – what's so interesting about that? And life in all the other American small towns as portrayed in literature. Isn't it enough simply to read all those fine books? What is there about them that still needs analysis? And why should it interest me in particular! Because I myself grew up near a small town? Small town sociology would be something else, something serious. But I don't understand the first thing about it. So I read old books and write a new one about them. It won't interest anyone.'

'What you're lacking is a sense of mission.'

'Quite right! But of course I'm carrying on. I can't simply give up.'

I could also have said: the end is in sight, I've got enough drafts and have already put together a first version of the complete text.

Presenting things as worse than they really are is something I'm good at.

My third summer here in my retreat. A good reason to write the definitive version at last, even if no one is waiting for it, never mind my hypersomnia or my lack of ambition.

It was nice of Anna to have asked. She herself is getting on as she should in her career, she'll be changing jobs in June, from Biel back to Zurich, senior physician in the Triemli district hospital. And she's got her FMH title now too. So there will be no more stopping by here anymore, it will probably be the end of her spontaneous visits.

What about the other matter? That long blue Monday, moonstruck in the morning, my own little story within the big story? Early morning memory training, that's what you could call it.

But what will I remember in ten years' time about things that are happening now, in the big story or in my own little one. In ten years' time, will I remember that a pope died this spring, that a new pope was elected? Or that Blair won the elections for the third time? Hardly.

And my third summer here in the Steingruben district? How a temporary arrangement grew into more than two years – yes, that's something that might linger in my memory.

3

'You can't lose what you never possessed ...'

If I spent every free minute at the typewriter, I might perhaps manage to finish the trilogy before the summer holidays. At least I'd have a first copy or, at the very least, all the necessary drafts.

I did no more than the absolute minimum for college, and occasionally I copied my homework from Oscar, something I'd never done before. Now was not the time for mathematics, geometry and such things, I could deal with all that again later. But my model schoolboy reflexes, at least, prevailed. I prepared for tests at the very last moment: my misery shouldn't be compounded by the mishap of a bad mark.

At first I got on well with the trilogy. At Whitsun with Whit Monday being a holiday, and then in the following week with Corpus Christi, there were days off school. I also gained time because I didn't have to make efforts any more to bring about chance meetings with Claudia. I also met Bede and his clique less often. I did continue to frequent Dornachia events, but the ball in Bad Attisholz at the end of May was off for me of course.

The ring file filled up with drafts, lists of themes and scenes, storylines, stage directions and the first dialogues. Soon, however, I noticed that it was difficult for me to invent dialogues, much more difficult than I'd imagined in my initial enthusiasm. Had I ever paid any attention before to how people talk to each other? The banal chatterings around me, and dialogues – real dialogues for the stage – were two completely different things. Sentences lingered in my mind, new sentences occurred to me, but only single sentences, not dialogues with replies and rejoinders.

As to writing monologues, it was something I managed reasonably well, albeit only after several attempts. Self-talk on my way home from town was something I was familiar with, and just recently, in the past few weeks, my experience had been refreshed. And then too, on that Saturday morning in Zurich, on my way to the station, I'd bought *Spoon River Anthology*, those voices of the dead spoken from the grave, retrospective accounts of lives in the small town, of individual small worlds, laconic, complex, angry, resigned, bitter, cool, astonished or hardened.

I'd insert such monologues into the plot like operatic arias. Monologues now, monologues then: the past and the present and a possible future would be boldly thrown together in disorder. Not only was that permitted, it was positively demanded by modern drama à la Thornton Wilder.

In the second week of June I decided to stay at home. The free Wednesday afternoons, the evenings, the

Saturday afternoons and the Sundays weren't sufficient. I wasn't getting on fast enough with the trilogy.

The residents of Spoon River are speaking from the grave when they set the record of their lives straight. I would set my record straight here and now. Everything that had ever crossed my mind concerning the Ganters and the Carrels, all the thoughts I'd ever had concerning my own life and life in general – all of it had to be put on stage. Now that I had the opportunity I couldn't let the chance escape, and if I didn't make headway I had to create the conditions that would let me work at it without interruption. I couldn't afford to go to town every day and sit through the hours at college.

Playing truant was not the right word for it.

I had another four weeks ahead of me before the holidays began.

What does someone like Claudia say to somebody like me if she doesn't want to offend him but still needs to say no? What does someone like Bede, seated at the round metal table of the open-air café, say to someone like Claudia, to someone like Elizabeth? What does a Paul Ganter sound like when he comes home late at night? Should the father's tirades be naturalistic, bombastic, sarcastic or perhaps sardonic? I'd have to reread Arthur Miller again and see how he has his salesman come home. And how shall I have the clique talk in the school corridor? How can I stage something like the Dornachia fraternity? I'd have to read it all up again in Wilder's *Our Town*.

College was out of the way, maths and French and German and geography and physics were out of the way. All those things were going on without me now. I had a typewriter and paper, I had the mornings, the afternoons, the evenings. I had my walks to Hazel Wood and back via Sagacker Heights. Towering clouds over green slopes, over yellowing slopes, fields of wheat in the late morning, in the early afternoon, fields of wheat in the evening.

There wasn't a moment to be lost, not a single idea must be lost, the plays had to be written, they should have been written long ago. Why hadn't I already hit on the idea in the winter? Perhaps that awful thing would never have happened. If I'd started on something like that in the winter, there'd have been less danger, I wouldn't have made such a fool of myself.

This was the only chance I had left. Soon the summer holidays would begin and I'd hardly written the first part of the trilogy. And what I had were mainly drafts, individual scenes in no dramatically convincing sequence.

Panic attack at the little table out on the landing. I rushed down the steps, past the dunghill and across the Furrers' drive. Nothing will come of it, nothing, it'll never come to anything, I can't do it. Why should someone like me manage to write a play? What did acting in a play and writing a play have to do with each other? What an idiot I was to have let myself in for it.

Along under the cherry trees towards Hazel Wood. Talk, talk, that isn't the problem, never was. You talk to yourself to reach a decision, you talk to yourself to work up courage, you apologise, you justify yourself, you work everything out beforehand, in the aftermath, for as long as you can remember you always have. You should be able to make something out of all that drivel, after all self-talk is also talk, and you manage monologues, don't you?

So get started, act yourself for a start, act what you're doing this very moment. You're walking along the beaten track to the road, behind you the woods, in front of you Sagacker Heights, down below to the right the roofs of Langendorf, eleven o'clock chimes up from the town, and here's Claudia coming towards you along the edge of the wheat field, unlikely as it might be that she should turn up here, that's the scene, that's how it occurs to you, take it as it is, improbable and wonderful, put the beaten track with the wheat field on the left and the barley field on the right into the backdrop and do what you do as though you were acting it, as though it was a role. Act the role well or badly, it doesn't matter, say spontaneously whatever comes to mind, justify yourself if you have to, express your annoyance if you feel annoyed, ask what you have to ask, ask carefully, brashly, beat about the bush or just keep talking. Claudia is standing in front of you in the middle of the wheat field, on the mound of the Crooked Tower, under the railway bridge, in the bicycle basement – does it matter where? It's easy to change the scenery, perform your idiot act, the way you performed it, it could have turned out differently, start somehow or other, spit it out, come on out with it! Never mind if it's all blabla, there has to be talk on stage, you can't have all those Claudias, Bedes, Elizabeths stand around with nothing to say. And even if you haven't got the text yet, act as if you'd already written the dialogue. You know what it's going to be about. The inevitable row? Start quarrelling. The big question? Why are you hesitating? Start asking. Play it like jazz, and whatever Jacob says about jazz, say it too, say what Claudia's sister says, say it out loud, speak here on this stage, even if you don't know the text by heart, even if the text hasn't even been written yet. Oh, Marlon Brando, James Dean, Paul Newman, stand by me!

In reviews of Elia Kazan's films I'd found hints on how actors in New York learned to immerse themselves in their roles. However, my knowledge of the Actors Studio method was very vague. But as long as the holidays hadn't begun, I didn't dare go into town and look for an article on it in the library. I had to make do with the little I knew. I used it to piece together a theory. I couldn't think of anything better. It had to help. And so it did to some extent.

4
'Your hair is like the wheatfield on the hill ...'

'... Your hair is like the wheatfield on the hill, and the wind blows through it ...'

Yet nothing about Claudia was bright, blonde, billowing, flowing, sweeping, nothing like that. On the contrary, her hair was brown, cut in a short pageboy, and she was slim, thin, almost wiry. Yet, of all things, I made a tall blonde out of her, I turned little boney Claudia into a girl with a mass of blonde hair, a Marilyn Monroe.

It must have been the wheatfields that prompted me, wheatfields that I saw like that for the first time that summer. They spoke to me, they told me something, even if I didn't understand exactly what. The sight of them moved me, and in my monologues the quiet, restrained power of those fields of golden ears became the girl's hair, a fetish, a daydream, a rapture.

Ears and ears of wheat, gusts of wind, the shimmering light, drifting cloud shadows, and I was part of the wind and simultaneously part of those wheatfields along the edge of Hazel Wood. Bede would probably have been able to give me the philosophical explanation even then: in motion with motion, flowing with the flow, at one with nature – something mystico-metaphysical along those lines.

But whatever it was, it was new, completely new for me. In all those years that I'd lived next to Furrers Farm, on seeing wheatfields, all I'd ever think of was work. After the reaper-binder had driven over the field, the sheaves would be lying in loose rows on the ground, and we boys stacked them into stooks so that the ears and the straw and the weeds that had been mown with the straw could dry in the July heat. A few days later the stooks would be pulled apart, and all over the field sheaves would be lying waiting to be picked up. Eagerly we thrust our forks into them and pitched them onto the waggon, onto the growing load. Still children, Ernst Furrer the same age as me, and Heinz his younger brother, we were proud to be doing men's work. One sheaf after the other, we heaved them up for Herr Furrer to place in such a way that the load would be as broad and as high as possible without falling apart on the way to the barn. We were proud that we had enough strength and endurance to load two or even three waggons in the heat of the afternoon.

But no more of the same that summer. The wheatfields had become something else for me. I didn't help the Furrers with the harvest, perhaps I'd help them again next year. No menial work that summer, not on a building site, nor farmwork for the Furrers. That summer there was only one job to be done, my main job.

The barley field down from the reservoir to the wood. The gossamer yellow of the bearded heads, a vast beige-coloured carpet:

'… a finely tufted carpet spread out before the throne of a nameless god …'

Apparently I wasn't embarrassed to write that kind of thing, there are lots of similar things to be found in the hero's monologues. The barley with its bearded heads had to serve to conjure up before my eyes the down on the nape of Claudia's neck, the fine down on Claudia's arms. Slopes and hills and hollows became the shapes of neck and shoulder and back.

For weeks I'd walked here every day through the fields. At the start of the long school holidays the fields had still been green, a strong bluish green. Then the green lightened, a yellowish, reddish, brownish glimmer came into the brightening green, still the smell was of lush vegetation. Not yet the fermented smell of ripe wheat as now, after the previous day's rain, when the sun was warming and drying the field again.

Forever in motion, alive, bending gently in fleeting waves, buffeted by the wind. But even when there was no wind, the play of shadow and light continued and, despite the calm, there was always a stirring somewhere, a slight quivering here, there, and there again, even when there was hardly a breath of wind to be felt.

The multitude of stalks, prodigiously uniform and at the same time prodigiously diverse; the single stalk in front of me, thin, delicate – and the vastness of the field; the single ear – and the millions of ears in the wheat field here and in the fields of wheat, barley and rye nearby. There was a message there, I sensed it vaguely.

It stirred me, and it soothed me. It drove me on and sometimes, for the duration of my breaktime walk, it made me feel relaxed and calm.

I'm trying to write down what I felt at the time and what occurred to me then. No, I'm trying to write down what comes to my mind now, more than forty years later, what comes to my mind when I'm transported back to those mornings and afternoons, what comes to mind here and now in the early morning when I recall those mornings and afternoons.

There are the scribblings in the notebooks. But can those scribblings be relied on? I wrote all of it down so as to make headway on the trilogy: every idea, however ridiculous, was worth registering, if only because I'd finally thought of something again. I'd skipped school in order to write the trilogy. I still hadn't reached my goal. I had to get ahead, so the least I could do was note down everything that occurred to me, even if the things that occurred to me were no good. Doing nothing at all when the trilogy had come to a standstill was out of the question. Keep at it, draw outlines of the sets, make lists of scenes, and what shall I make the stage manager say, part one, part two, finale presto, go through with it!

Anna rings up and inquires about Erica.

'Have you heard from her? Has she called you? The bombings. She's in London at the moment, isn't she?'

'No, no, luckily not. She's been up in Edinburgh since last Tuesday. And on her way there she took a taxi from Waterloo to King's Cross, so she never took the Tube.'

'How is she? What does she say?'

'Oh, she doesn't make much of it. But, of course, for the people in Edinburgh the attacks are a shock.'

'You see! If it happens in London it could also happen in Scotland. As for me, I'd be off at once, by train or by plane, straight back home as quickly as possible.'

'It's not what she's likely to do, she doesn't easily get worked up. But on the home journey she won't be staying in London long, she promised me that at least.'

Last year she was there the second week of July, I looked it up in my diary. And she took the Tube every day. She could have been there now, could have used the Tube.

By the skin of her teeth! Nonsense, she said, I needn't worry about her.

And here in our small town it's business as usual. I get up at five, and that summer comes back again and along with it the summer before that summer.

In the afternoons I'm in the reading room of the library, correcting what I've written on Anderson once more, paragraph by paragraph, chapter by chapter. The reading room is a good place for that, in the first weeks of the holidays I always find a seat, and anyway, if I wasn't here I'd just sleep the afternoons away.

Yesterday towards evening, as I crossed Loreto Meadows on my way home from the library, a combine harvester was drawing its tracks around the wheatfield. It was almost like in Anderson's *Winesburg* in distant America, fields and farmwork right next to the houses on the outskirts of the town. And it was almost like the scene between the edge of the woods and Sagacker Heights that summer.

5

'Out with it!'

All winter I'd been anxious to say as little as possible about my family. And now, all of a sudden, this mad urge to put it on display for Claudia to see. Defiantly, with the scenes out on the landing and in the kitchen and my father's midnight homecomings, I presented the disorderly house by the stream before her. A blustering father, a nagging mother and a cheeky sister made their big appearance.

Why was I dragging it out into the limelight right

now? Only on paper, admittedly, but with the aim of running to Claudia with the whole rigmarole as soon as it had all been written down. If no one else reads the three plays, at least Claudia will read them, she'll have to read them, who else are they being written for?

Claudia should get to know everything about the Ganters by the stream, and that wasn't possible without a minimum of self-exposure. If I showed her how I lived then, and how I lived now, she'd understand me; perhaps, belatedly, she'd finally come to understand: first my ridiculous shyness, then my annoying devotion, my mulishness, all the embarrassments I'd caused her. If I drew attention to those failings without sparing myself, mightn't she regard that as something that spoke in my favour, that justified me, at least partly, in her eyes? And the fact that I was writing a trilogy, wasn't that already a sign that I was somehow worthy of her, or at least that I might be someday in the future?

I can't find anything like that in my notes, but such thoughts must have gone through my head.

And had I ever thought of a performance, a real performance of the three plays? On the stage in the Kreuz, in the chaplaincy, in the concert hall in Langendorf or even in the assembly hall of the Kantonsschule. The author, the director, the stage manager, the leading actor, the set designer, the lighting technician, all in one person. With weeks of rehearsals, with a dress rehearsal and a premiere. Perhaps I could ask the same people who had rehearsed Camus' *The Just Assassins* the previous year in the forest glade. Of course Claudia wouldn't be there, but instead, this time there'd be Jacob; he'd take care of the music, the right medley of Goldberg Variations and jazz with a hint of Kurt Weill and several passages from American soundtracks. Bede, again, could supply the clever comments, freely adapted from Sartre, Marx, or Freud. And Elizabeth would be Claudia alias Margarita: with her blond shoulder-length mop of fuzzy hair she'd be the ideal casting.

It was particularly when I was brooding over some dialogue without making headway that such thoughts went through my head.

And certainly on that terrible day too – it must have been the second week of the holidays – when I read through the drafts of each of the three plays systematically for the first time. Despondency is too weak a word for it. All my rounds to Hazel Wood, Sagacker Heights and back to Furrers Farm, nothing helped.

Yet I had to pick myself up again. Those dialogues can surely be improved. It's not important that the sentences follow each other in an orderly pattern, question, answer, question. What matters is that I should make some discovery in the process. The sentences should lead me on to something I didn't know beforehand, they should show me something I hadn't seen before. That's what they're there for, that's why I'm writing them down, that's why I'm stringing them together. They don't have to be to my liking, they don't have to be to anyone's liking. All I'm trying to find out by writing them down is how a simple love story could turn into such a calamity.

An evening that remained in my memory: I'd eaten too much and felt slightly sick. That often happened and can't be the reason I kept remembering it. But it was not only my stomach that was full that evening, I was also filled with irritation at not being able to work properly because I felt sick, and so the evening was lost as far as continuing with my work was concerned.

Then I remembered my Dornachia friends: how they used to vomit after they'd drunk too much beer, how they made themselves throw up, and how they felt much better afterwards. I'd already helped Bede do it, once in the park with the aviary behind the cathedral, and once down by the Aare. Mightn't a thing that helps you when you've drunk too much beer also help when you've overeaten? I had to get my stomach empty again. Then I'd feel lighter, I'd be able to write all evening and into the night.

On the banks of the stream amid elder and willow no one would see me. I stuck a blade of grass into my mouth and tried to touch the tonsils at the back of my throat with it.

Down in the wash house I rinsed the sourish remains of potato out of my mouth and drank some cold water. Mashed potatoes, cheesy potatoes or boiled potatoes? With stewed plums or with salad? I'd gobbled it up without paying attention. On a peaceful Sunday evening, my father was there, my younger sister was there.

I'd never made myself vomit before. But I had to finish off my long blue Monday, I had to write the fair copy of those three plays, type them out in one last final effort. I had to deliver the pile of paper to Claudia the following week or, at the very latest, the week after that. Yes, that's what I'd do. I'd have a plausible reason for going to town and ringing the bell at the house on the Aare.

A hero's life indeed!

6

'When we meet again in ten years time ...'

After the end of the summer holidays I waited day after day, week after week for some kind of sign from Claudia. When I'd brought her the trilogy she hadn't seemed surprised. She would read the plays, she said kindly, and then she'd get in touch.

Days passed, weeks passed, life at the Kantonsschule continued as usual. For six months I'd done no more than the bare minimum. Next spring there would be a couple of important exams and I'd neglected my maths and French for months, so now I had to catch up.

Late summer was over, it was already autumn. Again and again I resolved to ring the Carrels or to watch out for Claudia in the long break or after school. However, when once I saw her come out of the gym and go across to Fegetzallee I didn't do anything. Something kept me back. Was it pride? Was it defiance? I'd done what had to be done, I couldn't do more, and now I didn't want to do anything more.

I'd waited in vain for so long that I'd pretty well resigned myself to the fact that nothing would happen.

I remember the day, it was a Monday, the Monday of the second week after the autumn holidays. As I came out of the bicycle cellar I found Claudia standing at the top of the ramp. She was holding a carrier bag in her hand, and I immediately recognised it as the bag I'd brought her the trilogy in.

'This is yours,' she said. 'Sorry, I should have given it back to you a long time ago.'

And what else did she say? I don't remember. It can't have been much.

I see myself sitting on the bed in my den under the roof. I'm holding the three ring binders in my hands. No letter, no note, not a single handwritten comment in the margin of a page.

I left the house, crossed the Furrers' forecourt, went through the orchard, went through the falling darkness towards Hazel Wood.

I was standing on the mound of the reservoir.

'That's the end,' I heard myself say – softly, as you do when you're talking to yourself. I pitied myself for having to utter that sentence. It did me good to utter that sentence. It was like at the theatre, it wasn't meant seriously. I knew that the whole thing had only been an act.

When I try to remember further scenes of despondency I can't think of anything.

But four or five weeks later I moved out of home. I found a room in town. Katherine would advance me the money for the rent. In barely one and a half years I'd be out of college, I'd be a teacher and earn enough to be able to pay her the money back.

You can commit suicide. Or you can rent a room in town.

The lunacy of youth.

223

Outlandish though it was, the idea of death had comforted me, it had depressed me and comforted me at the same time. It meant I had a choice again, I could do something, or I could let something be. The idea proved just how downhearted I was. It provided a solid ground, it gave me a kind of earnestness in that fools' play. And there was a reaction too: that's enough now, enough of all that! I've been on the wrong track. I tried everything, nothing worked out. I always knew it vaguely, now I know for sure.

What are you collecting those memories for? What's the use? Bye-bye, you'll be dying soon anyway. After the age of sixty it's something you can tell yourself every day!

Indeed, what's another twenty years at that age? A few easy years if you're lucky, many trying years if things go the other way.

But one thing is clear at least: If you decided to recall that story in twenty years time, by then it would definitely be too late to gain any new insights. In twenty years time there'd be no sense in recalling those old stories.

And what's the sense now? Not much sense, no doubt, but it does seem to give you some pleasure.

Will that do for a reason? I can think of no better.

X

SUCCESSORS

'… I tried to leave you behind me, but I am more faithful than
I intended to be!'

Tennessee Williams, *The Glass Menagerie*

1

Maria, Madeleine,
Verena, Veronica

Love and passion: the end. And four months later, back
again. It happened so swiftly, it began so easily.

Needless to say, unrequited passion once more! Was
it bad? A new attack? The nice thing about it was that,
once again, it was passion.

Maria was her name, she was in the class below mine
and in no way less unique than Claudia had been. She
caught my eye at the end of January during the college
ski camp in Stoos.

Dances at the camp – in the two previous years I'd
seldom taken part in those capers. In my first year I'd
hardly dared, and in the second year the only person I'd
have had eyes for would have been a dancing Claudia –
and she, being a student at the Gymnasium, wasn't there.

Students at the teacher training college all had to
learn to play an instrument, so there were always enough
people who could also play dance music. This time it
was a band from the second year: trumpet, clarinet, cello
and drums. 'Criminal Tango', Bechet's 'Petite Fleur',
variations on Gershwin's 'Summertime', and hits from
films were popular.

I watched the goings-on. It was much the same as at
the evening entertainments in the Kreuz in Oberdorf:

The girls waited to be asked to dance. They could turn you down. Some dancers were often asked, others seldom.

I was not the only one to be struck by Maria. A vivacious mop of curls, not pale slim and lanky, but buxom, radiant, a bundle of energy, a marvellously nimble little dancer.

She seemed to be amused that I kept asking her to dance.

After the skiing holidays I invited her to the town theatre to see Ibsen's *A Doll's House*. There was no stroll through the town afterwards, no long walk together along the banks of the Aare: Maria lived in the Girls' Hostel, in the Palais Besenval, only a couple of paces away from the theatre.

From the beginning, everything went much faster than with Claudia. I didn't dither. I'd moved out of home, become independent, and had thus done something no one else in my college year had done. That was something new, it was exhilarating. The fact that Katherine was paying my rent was a slight blot; however it was something I could ignore: the unfortunate situation wouldn't last long, soon I'd be a teacher and my salary would be high enough to pay everything back. Going up to Oberdorf for supper two or three times a week was also something that didn't really fit in with my new-found independence; however it was acceptable. Most of the time I lived on porridge oats, yoghurt, jam, and bread, and all my mother's remonstrations that my parsimonious diet was unhealthy couldn't make me change.

Due to a shortage of teachers, several students were

sent out on three-week supply jobs. Towards the end of May I found myself standing alone in front of a class for the first time, in Trimbach.

It was then, too, that my story with Maria came to an end.

This time I didn't have to write a play. A couple of strolls along the Aare were enough. When the Dornachia dance event on Lake Aeschi came up I invited a classmate.

The job in Trimbach came in very handy. I was glad for the pay. I wanted to depend as little as possible on my sister's money.

And that first supply job wasn't to be the last. The teacher shortage increased as autumn approached. More than twenty students were allowed to leave college six months earlier than envisaged. I was one of them. No one had noticed that I'd long ago stopped being the model student I once was.

Mümliswil behind the mountain, my first winter. I still went to town quite often: down to Balsthal by bike, then through the Klus Gorge to Oensingen where I got on the train. Cinema, theatre, library. I also went to the Dornachia do's.

Now it was Madeleine who got invited. For a time I wrote her a letter every week. Being a young schoolmaster far away on the other side of the mountain turned out to be an advantage: it gave me a convincing excuse to write letters. It was something I still found easier than talking.

In those letters there was never any mention of love. I

wrote about the films we'd seen together, about the books I was reading. I told Madeleine the things I heard in the Schweizerhalle or in the Ochsen whenever I met colleagues there for lunch: good Catholic sanctimoniousness and the corresponding minor scandals.

I wrote the letters in my classroom, as most evenings I stayed in the school until ten. As it happened, my letter-writing contributed greatly to my soon gaining a reputation as a dutiful teacher. Way beyond the village, the light in the windows of my classroom could be seen advertising my diligence, my conscientiousness, my reliability.

Madeleine seldom wrote back.

March came, April followed, grass grew, sap rose in trees, greenness all around advertised hope. The benches had been set up again in the town parks and on the mound of the Crooked Tower. But it was over with Madeleine. There was no point in holding it against her.

At the end of May there was a colleague from Matzendorf. Her name was Verena. It was the beginning of a bewildering summer. Veronica, a red-headed, white-skinned, quick-to-blush doctor's assistant from Balsthal replaced the colleague from Matzendorf. I regretted the swap, for now there was someone continually pestering me to go dancing, no weekend without some kind of party organised by the choral club, the sports club, the brass-band.

What was it like? Do I really have to recall all the details? Two weeks of the summer holidays with other flirts, and then I had to go away to do my military training.

2
An Attack or an Affair?

After my return from military training in the middle of November, my second winter in Mümliswil.

Beat Hug, a colleague who had completed his training as a second-lieutenant during the summer, introduced a new pastime. Social life behind the mountain began to flourish, I didn't need the town in front of the mountain any more. No discussions now about Camus, Sartre, Nietzsche, Marx or the like, we didn't even talk about films: women provided us with more than enough material for conversation.

Beat had already bought himself a car – which was an exception for novice teachers at the time, but he lived with his parents in Dulliken and needed the car for the long commute to his work. Now the car was also used for expeditions to the dance halls in the adjacent cantons – Solothurn still didn't have that kind of place. We drove up to Langenbruck or across to Aarau, occasionally to Basel too.

Cherchez la femme. It was a gamble with the odds at one to ten, and cooperation between us always verged on competition. In which case, however complicitous we might be, any trick could be used to outmanoeuvre the other. For if, on such occasions, we met girls we liked, we had to make a date as soon as possible: cinema, dance, fondue. I often had to fiddle around with bus and train timetables, but Beat with his car had an advantage, and two thirds of the times he emerged victorious.

Anyhow he always won the more attractive women, while I made do with plainer ones, which also meant that if nothing came of it – which was often the case – I wasn't so upset.

It didn't take much to fall in love. It was almost enough for the person to be female. Puppies play with balls of wool, with sticks or rubber balls as if they were their own kind. And we would have liked to play with our new conquests as if they were balls of wool or rubber balls. However, things seldom went far – a private striptease was breathtaking enough.

If not this one, then the next; an arm around her shoulders, around her waist, a kiss on the neck just below the ear, followed by the rest. Short stories with Verenas, Veronicas, Linas and Lenas, whoever, it hardly made a difference.

Admittedly in the beginning they were all a bit like Claudia. But in the meantime I'd acquired the gift of the gab: at times you just have to take the plunge, it's up to you to decide, it's okay to hesitate but better to reach a decision and see what comes of it, what do you think I'm thinking, praise her plumpness or her boniness, the colour of her eyes, really I like you, no, don't talk, or yes, out with it, a long time, wait a minute, how long, never dared to do anything because I was thinking, how will it turn out, what's starting now … That kind of thing.

My second summer behind the mountain, my third winter. I went to Zurich frequently now, and occasionally I met Bede there. He was doing German and Philosophy; he took me along to lectures a couple of times, we dined in the students' canteen, or we strolled through the Niederdorf district.

Sitting in the railway station buffet leafing through a book. Looking up discreetly from time to time, who was I looking out for? Behind a glass of beer, a cigarette in the corner of my mouth, the newly bought book in my hand, I felt able to cope with any vicissitudes. Hunting down happiness with a shotgun. Those streets, trams, houses, the people inside them, they manage without me, I manage without them. What does it matter!

The long winters behind the mountain, the summers behind the mountain, the springs, the autumns, and with each season the beginnings and endings of holidays, the days off for Saint Nicholas, Christmas, New Year, Carnival, the weekends that started on Saturday afternoon, and the Sunday evenings that followed – a permanent merry-go-round, a relay race in which I was the runner and also the baton. Want breeds want, somewhere there was a void, not found, not filled.

Lena, the bookseller. My third winter behind the mountain, it would be my last. But it wasn't in Olten or in Zurich that I first met Lena, it was in Solothurn.

I still went to town once every three or four weeks, usually on a Saturday afternoon. There was no decent library behind the mountain and I enjoyed spending an afternoon in the reading room of the Central Library; this was always followed by a visit to the bookshop to buy one of the books I'd just read a review of in *Du* or in the *Neue Zürcher Zeitung*.

Lena had already caught my eye that summer. But in spite of all my book buying it was a long time before a suitable opportunity arose. It was difficult to know if her smile and her efficiency in dealing with my book orders were intended for me as a customer or for me as a person.

She hesitated before accepting my first invitation, the next time she turned me down. A few weeks later I was in favour again. Why exactly? I never really knew.

She looked like a Renoir woman, plump all over. And exuberant to match. As a bather, her pale brown hair tied up on her head, her beige-yellow skin, almost hairless, silky.

She'd changed jobs often, she'd only been working here for a year. Her previous boyfriend had apparently been tormenting himself with the idea of suicide, not because of her, but out of a general feeling of anguish. Although he didn't require her to follow him, he wanted her to help him. They'd had stormy times. Now with me she could relax, she said.

She had a tendency to talk about the meaning of life at the slightest provocation. Which easily led on to thoughts about death. An afterlife was out of question: she'd read too much to believe in that. The only thing that would survive at the end of the day was what she did here and now. And selling books wasn't really enough. A place in people's memories, in mine for example: it was something I was happy to offer her.

My fascination didn't last long. Three years before, Claudia had seemed to be like that: her slender head like a flickering flame rising from the metaphysical darkness, enlightening, disturbing, transforming everything. Now such a woman, a chain-smoker, was seated on my bed, in long suede boots, fine-stockinged, and I had a nasty feeling that I wasn't mustering up enough gratitude.

When I found body lice, but she found none, the metaphysics became too much for me. We separated, not without pain. That was the least that could be expected from life.

It was high time for a change: no third summer behind the mountain, a first one in Winznau instead, no fourth winter far away behind the mountain, but a first one back in a region where there were other diversions on offer.

Not that there was much going on in Olten, let alone in Winznau. However, Zurich was within easy reach now, and trains for the home journey ran until midnight. No more changing trains and waiting in the draughty station in Olten, no more long nocturnal cycle rides from Oensingen through the narrow gorge to the other side of the mountain, no more cycling through the rain and the cold, no more rain-drenched clothes, no need any more for two alarm clocks to tear me out of my short sleep on Saturday mornings.

The reason I gave for changing my job was that I wanted to attend some lectures at the university in Zurich, which would be difficult while I was living in Mümliswil; I said I intended to become a secondary school teacher.

To my surprise they were reluctant to let me go. Admittedly, I'd never aspired to stand out as a bad teacher. I'd continued to spend many evenings in the classroom. Of course I occasionally corrected essays and dictations there or prepared my lessons for the following days, or wrote things up on the blackboard. But that only accounted for a fraction of the time I spent there. Most often I read books that had no bearing at all on school matters. Or I listened to one of the many radio plays that I'd recorded over the years. I'd recorded them with a Revox tape recorder that I'd bought for my first Christmas behind the mountain.

A roof, a gutter, two stockinged feet, the snow rails over to the chimney. My pullover was thrown out after me and the window hastily shut.

All around, the grey morning and slippery tiles and autumn. Crouched down behind the chimney, I held still and let the two women inside potter around. Out here I was safe. It couldn't take long for the flat to be cleaned.

Another Verena-Veronica story, come to a dramatic climax up on the roof. Was this affair with my colleague Ruth perhaps an example of my fresh start in front of the mountain?

Sloping roofs, jumbled buildings, aerials in the foggy grey. The afternoon would have been a more agreeable time to be sitting there behind the chimney. I heard the window being opened again, and saw a hand shaking the dust from a duster. Through the open window I could hear talking from within, two women's voices, and I pictured them: Ruth standing in the doorway, a half finished cup of coffee in her hand, keeping a watch on the other woman; eyes following the duster, the mop, she assures herself that there's nothing still lying around on the chest of drawers, by the bed or beside the wardrobe, that might belong to a man, the man out on the roof.

Ruth didn't want to be caught out, it was understandable. She didn't want to have to introduce her colleague from Winznau to her aunt so early in the morning. Whether he was a colleague or not, the studio flat, furnished, had been let to a single person.

I watched the pigeons, not thinking of anything much, carefully trying now and then to find a more comfortable position for my legs. A few roofs away, a woman with a basin appeared and hung up the washing without looking across in my direction.

Could the Carrels' house be seen from here? How much better off I was now – in spite of my exposed situation – than the Romeo of those days! All I had to do was admit it. Safely crouched behind the broad chimney, I could wait until a hand round the metal dormer waved me in.

Ruth, taciturn, obstinate, brow-wrinkling, mouth-twitching; Ruth who had landed herself in an awkward situation thanks to me. Now she poured us another cup of coffee, and we continued the breakfast we'd had to interrupt so very abruptly. She grumbled about her aunt: 'Why did she have to come today of all days, why not tomorrow or the day after, as she usually does?'

Colleagues, again and again. Female creatures I was familiar with, more or less. Go on, get moving, along the well-worn track! With them I had a fair chance of gaining a slight feeling of superiority – both reassuring and stimulating.

Occasionally it was difficult to distinguish between an attack of Clauditis and a Verena-Veronica affair. Usually the attack would turn into an affair, affairs seldom turned into attacks. But that happened too.

And what about Ruth? How and when had it started with Ruth?

In those days there was so much happening at the same time, all pell-mell, that it's easy for me to get the chronology wrong. It was at the Cantonal Teachers Conference, I remember. It must have been my first summer in Winznau, sometime between the summer and autumn holidays. In a marquee somewhere or other in the Bucheggberg district; a festival – music, yodel or gymnastics – had been held there shortly before, and the teachers' union had availed itself of the chance to use the erected marquee for its own big annual event.

Ruth was sitting diagonally opposite me. Her slim throat, her short hair, the way she sat there, stretched, then looked behind her a first time.

An attack, no doubt about it.

The attic flat in the Goldgasse. The house belonged to her aunt. Since her niece was fully occupied, what with her sideline playing the organ, the aunt offered her weekly cleaning besides affordable housing. That might have been convenient. However it soon became apparent that her aunt was all too keen on cleanliness – the floor, the laundry, morals.

Gentleman visitors, in particular, led to complications.

That's how I landed up on the roof on that Monday morning. It was in the first week of the autumn holidays.

Then we escaped from her aunt's surveillance and drove through the Val de Travers to France. Ruth had a car, a Citroën Diane. We spent our first night in Pontarlier. Then Châlon-sur-Saône, Mâcon. Swarms of birds plummeted down into the plane trees. Traffic thundered down the riverside road. Hills ribbed with rows of vines. And wherever Ruth saw a church we had to go and look at it. Twice she even managed to get permission to play the organ. Abandoned pastures behind Cluny, remoteness, hotel rooms, half empty restaurants.

After that week in France, Ruth came to see me every week in Winznau Marsh. She always parked her car up in the village and walked down to the Marsh on foot.

I wasn't unhappy with the situation. A colleague who was good at playing the organ: that impressed me. There was something about this Ruth that fascinated me. Advent again. Waiting for what? For whom? Why waiting? During the week it was teaching as usual, including the rehearsals for a big nativity play. Once a week I went to Zurich. The weekends were filled with all kinds of cultural activities. Since getting to know Ruth I frequently went to concerts.

I was saved by the fact that long-legged, slender-necked Ruth only paid attention to inner qualities, that she generally dressed plainly and that she chewed her nails. For if there hadn't been all manner of things I could secretly criticise her for, I'd have been at her mercy.

Kinsey and Kamasutra, inner qualities remain invisible, someone like Ruth would have been best for a jealous man, not even visible when playing the organ. In that Advent season no one could have foreseen that only a year later she'd have been radically transformed by make-up and fashionable accessories.

3

Chaos

So many things were going on all over the place, it was as if life had been a perpetual round of entertainments in those days. I attended lectures in Zurich, sat in here and there. Bede had given me the idea. Perhaps I'd really take up studies. But there was no hurry.

Bede took me along to his select circle. After his youthful excesses with Nietzsche, Freud, Sartre and Marx, he'd come to Husserl and Heidegger. The meetings took place every few weeks, usually in the flat of a senior student who was already running a psychology practice. Back to the things themselves via eidetic reduction, from the logical investigations to transcendental consciousness. My contribution to those learned discussions was limited to that of an astonished listener. However I liked the academic aspect, even if it was just another form of entertainment.

I went to Zurich almost every week, and I usually ate in the university canteen. It was here that I first met Monica, a future remedial teacher who had previously been a teacher in the Zurich Oberland. She was five years older than I, and I wasn't quite sure if I should take the first step. There was Ruth, and Monica knew it.

Being no more than friends with Monica was easy. We drank coffee together, occasionally we went to the pictures or to an exhibition in the Kunsthaus, or we met at the theatre, and we even met once or twice in her small flat on Stauffacherplatz for a cup of tea. It went no further, things stayed like that until the end of the semester.

One Saturday afternoon – after a long pause – I went to the cinema with Monica again. It was the five o'clock session, I remember: an English film, a revival, *Room at the Top.* Just before the lights dimmed I noticed a slim head in one of the front rows, and during the credits, as people were beginning to stand up, I noticed the slim head again.

It was Claudia.

On the way out we met. Our conversation was short; I introduced Monica to her, she introduced Monica and me to her companion.

That's how I got to know Heinrich.

That evening, Monica had arranged to meet a few of her friends in the Bodega in the Niederdorf; I went with her. Thanks to the din there and amid the general elation, no one noticed how quiet I was. Twice we moved on to another pub. A young American suggested organising a midnight spaghetti party and invited us to his place. I'd stopped consulting my watch, the last train to Olten had left long since. There wouldn't be another train before Sunday morning, now it was already two a.m.

On foot to Stauffacherplatz, just the two of us again now. In Monica's kitchen, when she asked me what had struck me silent, I came out with it.

I told her the whole story with all the preludes and the postscripts, told her about that summer, about the many summers and winters that followed, about Maria, Madeleine, about Lindas and Lenas, Verenas, Veronicas. So that I missed the first train I'd meant to wait for while drinking coffee and chatting. I also missed a few more trains, and didn't return to Olten and Winznau Marsh until the afternoon.

Something strange had happened: Monica and I had finally managed to move on from simple camaraderie to a love affair. That was the kind of impact Claudia Carrel still had.

A Clauditis attack with Monica? From the very beginning, hardly a chance. Monica's robust body reminded me all too vividly of something more delicate. Only for a brief moment did those old stories and Monica's warm understanding manage to create the soft, wistful mood out of which big feelings grow. There could be no talk of erotic aura or verve.

Ruth in Solothurn and Monica in Zurich. As long as Ruth was the girlfriend who came to see me regularly in Winznau and with whom I regularly went to concerts, and as long as Monica was the friend I saw once a month in Zurich and with whom I could chat unreservedly, the one didn't interfere with the other, on the contrary. Now, all of a sudden, Claudia's appearance brought complications.

But hadn't it been true for some time now that the prospect of a visit from Ruth hardly filled me with eager anticipation? And hadn't I tried to find plausible excuses a couple of times recently when she'd wanted to take me to a concert? Although the attraction was still there, everything had become rather routine.

On the other hand, the affair with Monica was new. And she gave me a chance to stay in contact with Claudia. The two had been introduced to each other, they both lived near Stauffacherplatz, and they liked each other. With Monica as my girlfriend, I'd occasionally see Claudia.

When I told Ruth what had happened – the chance meeting with my old sweetheart and the odd sequel – she didn't think it was funny and she didn't think it had been purely by chance. She accused me of having deceived her all winter, there was no use my denying it, those lectures at the university, Bede et cetera, they were simply a pretext, in any case, she'd never heard me say anything about a remedial teacher. It was perfectly clear to her now why I hadn't wanted to go to the concert at the Great Minster in January. And anyway she didn't see any point in talking about it any more, or in talking to me any more for that matter.

Claudia and her friend Heinrich. He was a medical student from Germany, in Zurich since the previous autumn. He was hard-working and competent, one of the best, which is why he'd been able to come to Zurich for two semesters on a scholarship from Schleswig-Holstein.

The big house on Zweierstrasse, all the rooms rented out to students. Claudia and Heinrich lived on the top floor with three others. The roof terrace above them was often used in the summer. People went up there to sit in the sun, to read, to drink coffee. Evenings on the warm tin roof, the panoramic view over the neighbouring roofs.

Heinrich was the eldest child of a village schoolteacher. He'd grown up in a schoolhouse near Brunsbüttel on the Elbe. His father had wanted to be a physicist, had started university in Hamburg when the war interrupted his career. Up until six months before the end of the twelve-year Reich he served as a driver for officers in the general staff, always on the Western Front, in Holland, in France. During his first leave he got married. However, family life didn't start until two years after the end of the war: it was already 1947 by the time he came back to the Elbe after having been a prisoner of war in Marseille. During the war – in spite of or because of the war – he'd become the father of three children, and couldn't continue his studies in Hamburg. He took a crash training course and became a schoolteacher.

Right from the beginning, Heinrich acted as his father's assistant. It was a village school: there was only one big, very long classroom with the smaller children in the front rows, the bigger ones behind, forty or fifty children in all. The teacher's family lived in the school building, on the first floor.

A village near Brunsbüttel on the mouth of the Elbe – the Wadden Sea, dykes and marshland, and most of the village names ended in -husen, -büttel, -stedt or -koog. Everything desolate and flat and, on summer days, occasionally vast and beautiful.

Up on the tin roof on Zweierstrasse Heinrich told me about it. He was interested to learn that I myself was teaching in a small village, and that there was a canal that passed the village, and that on either side of the canal there were dams on which you could walk over to the next village. He also knew everything about the joys and pains of village schoolteachers, he liked talking, he talked a lot and I enjoyed listening to him. It was easy to get to know him.

The things he told me sounded familiar and at the same time unfamiliar. Everyday school life was something I was familiar with, but the everyday school life he'd experienced shortly after the war was unfamiliar – paper shortage, shortage of books, shortage of chalk, shortage of everything. It was my first time talking to a German who'd experienced the time immediately following the war, who'd experienced it living in a school, that is, in an environment I knew well.

Summer evenings on the tin roof.

Once, Claudia and Heinrich invited people to a pizza, there were other students there too, men and women. Monica and I provided the wine.

It was pleasant to be there. It was pleasant to see Claudia without having to talk to her, without having to undertake anything. I was glad everything went so uneventfully, was glad that everything was so normal, had become so marvellously normal.

A normalisation, that's what it must have been. I could show Claudia that I was like the others, not a spoilsport or a clumsy fool. I could show that I wasn't like I used to be, that over-the-top behaviour was no longer to be feared from me, that I could talk about harmless things, that I had a steady girlfriend. No more adolescent craziness, it was all over and done with, I now strode through life light of step, almost nonchalantly.

What were the subjects of conversation up there on the roof, down in the kitchen and in Heinrich's big room? Heinrich and Claudia talked about medicine, internships, past holidays, holiday plans. Heinrich and I talked about village schools, village schoolmasters, dykes, locks, the Wadden Sea and the Halligen islands, about the World War, about my military refresher courses in Entlebuch, in Basel-Landschaft, about community service in lieu of military service in Germany and the special opportunities for medical students, about war films, *All Quiet on the Western Front, The Bridge on the River Kwai, The Longest Day.* All in all, we talked a lot about films, hardly ever about the theatre and plays.

I only went to Zweierstrasse three or four times that early summer. Yet it appears to me now as if I was up there on the roof nearly every week. The evening we used a garden hose to lay a pipeline up to the terrace, so as to cool the roof and the flat beneath. It had been Heinrich's idea.

'You told me how things were. I think I understood you. In any case I made an effort. But why talk about effort, it was no trouble. You're really quite bearable, I wouldn't have thought it. Except that you bite my head off at the slightest thing – trifles, you have to admit it. If something's annoying you, say so. And when you're in a bad mood – as you so often are these days – don't take it out on me. It's not fair. And pointless too, as it happens.'

246

Monica's words. Others before her could have said the same. Monica fought back. I was annoyed with myself, and vented my annoyance on her.

Before my renewed encounter with Claudia, my relationship with Monica hadn't been a love affair. Then it had turned into a kind of attack. But it would hardly have lasted more than two or three weeks if it hadn't been for Claudia and her friend Heinrich, and if Monica hadn't got on so well with Claudia. Was Monica jealous of Claudia? She assured me she was not. I almost believed her. Was I jealous of Heinrich? It didn't upset me that Heinrich and Claudia were a couple. That, too, could almost be believed. That irksome matter from the past had been settled. With Monica as my girlfriend, my relationship with Claudia was almost as uncomplicatedly platonic as my relationship with Monica had been while Ruth was still visiting me regularly in Winznau Marsh.

Cool scheming on my part? More likely confused, undecided, cowardly. I had no idea what would become of it. That was one reason why my affair with Monica lasted so long, it must have been something like love after all.

When Monica began planning joint summer holidays, however, I began to feel uneasy. She suggested going to Spain. She had friends there.

I should have been glad, and I tried to get used to the idea of our spending holidays together, for there was no good reason against it. After all, the previous autumn the idea of touring Burgundy with Ruth hadn't sent me into a panic either.

Neither was it panic now. I was simply reluctant.

And what was the result? While Monica was visiting her friends in Spain I booked a last minute week in London with the Swiss Student Travel Agency, and by my second day there regretted not having gone on holiday with Monica.

So we made up again. I took the first step. It was easy to make it up with Monica, she wasn't someone to harbour a grudge.

Once, she took Heinrich and Claudia to Winznau in her car. We walked through the village. I gave Heinrich a tour of the school building. We took a long walk on the canal bank, and came back along the Old Aare. Heinrich and Claudia would soon be going to North Germany for a couple of weeks.

The affair with Monica continued, prosaic, mundane, normal.

I felt uneasy about it. But I couldn't bring myself to make a change.

Perhaps that was the reason for the relapse with Ruth.

It wasn't the Cantonal teachers conference this time, it was a Saturday afternoon in town. Since starting work on his dissertation, Bede was again to be found regularly in the reading room of the library. This time he hadn't only marked his pitch with two or three books as before, he'd arranged a complete working area for himself. However, he still didn't in the least mind being disturbed in his serious work.

And it was here one day in the reading room that I saw Ruth.

We had a cup of coffee in the Chutz. She didn't live in her aunt's house in the old town any more, she'd moved to a new block of flats in the Schützenmatt quarter.

And there'd been other changes too since our parting in the spring. Already in the library I'd noticed that Ruth wasn't wearing the nondescript clothes I'd known her for: now everything about her was elegant, her boots, her stockings, her skirt, her blouse, her sweater, and also her discreet make-up. The only thing that was still the same was her very short hair style. She said she was often in Olten again, she'd been asked to play the organ in St Martins Church.

This new Ruth was irresistible. At least this time I summoned up enough courage to inform Monica at once. And she seemed to be almost relieved. As if I'd become a burden, what with all my about-turns and half-measures.

'What? Your first love did medicine?'

'Eventually, yes. And her boyfriend those days was a medical student too. A German, in Zurich for two semesters, a good fellow, suited her better than I had a couple of years before when we were still at the Kantonsschule.'

'That means you kept in contact with her.'

'No, no, I just happened to bump into her again in Zurich.'

'When you were at university?'

'I hadn't started yet, I was still teaching in Winznau. But since when do daughters take an interest in their fathers' old love stories? The stories that happen around

249

you are sure to be much more interesting, *Dr House, Grey's Anatomy,* you know the TV stuff. If only a quarter of it's true, it shows that all kinds of things happen in hospitals.'

'Don't try to sidetrack me. We're not talking about hospital affairs, we're talking about your old flame. By the way, we read the true, real *Love Story* at school, with your colleague Brutschin.'

'And then?'

'Most of us liked it. As for me, I found it rather kitsch.'

'A true melodrama, isn't it? The whole trashy grief schedule in the opening sentences: "What can you say about a twenty-five-year-old girl who died? That she was beautiful. And brilliant. That she loved Mozart and Bach. And the Beatles. And me …" and so on and so forth.'

'Is that really the beginning? Fancy you still being able to recite that by heart!'

'Did you say still?'

'Oh, stop your Alzheimer jokes, I hear enough of them every day.'

'Yes, Segal with his best-seller, immediately turned into a film, with a sequel too. Ideally suited for English literature classes. There's hardly a more brilliant way popular fiction could be written, simply marvellous.'

'You're being satirical.'

'Am I? Perhaps, a little. It was always easy to appeal to pupils with Segal's *Love Story*. Easier at least than with one of Anderson's stories.'

4

Relapse

In Winznau Marsh, while I was sleeping through the Christmas holidays, I finally made a renewed effort to change my life. The period between Christmas and the New Year was a good time for it. On my walks along the canal and the Old Aare I came to the conclusion that it would be easiest to bring about a change if I put myself in a new situation. Simply changing jobs again wouldn't do.

Should I go to university like some of my classmates from the training college? One of them was doing maths in Bern, two others were doing the course for secondary school teachers. But I was a teacher already. Why go to university for three or four years, only to be a teacher again? Not a very tempting option! I considered the subjects taken by the people in the house on Zweierstrasse: Heinrich and Claudia's medical studies, on the same floor there was a Danish woman doing architecture, and a chemistry student who'd been a butcher before taking his Matura exams. And what about the floor below? Architecture, law, forestry and history.

As a model pupil I'd never really had a favourite subject. Something had to be learned, and I got good marks: that was enough to inspire mild interest. Only drama had for a while aroused greater interest, interest of a different kind. Yes, had, in the past tense: for my inclination and urge to appear on stage had also dwindled. By now I was managing without roles I'd committed to memory. The only plays I staged now were school plays. And while I was thus again brooding over what, if at all, I should study at university, Bede had already been working on his doctor's thesis in the Central Library reading room for months, and was nearly finished. Mightn't that also have been a sign? Like everything Bede did, it impressed me. The Concept of Nature in the Work of Adalbert Stifter, or Moonshine in Romantic Literature, or Content and Form of *The Glass Menagerie*, or The Significance of X in the Work of Y. But why me? Why should I concern myself with such things? And anyway, did I really need to be enrolled at a university to change my life? For it was clear: something had to change. Reasonably good teaching and now and then a half-hearted love affair – things couldn't go on in the same old routine.

So university after all, I couldn't think of anything else. Hand in my notice for the coming spring so as to become a secondary school teacher in Zurich. That was nothing special, it was modest, it was normal, an excellent reason, no school board could possibly find anything suspicious about it. And once I'd enrolled at the university I could still do whatever I fancied, in due time I'd know what that was. English? History? Simply get started, at worst with pedagogy – and why not? Bede also had pedagogy as his third subject, so there must be something in it.

Sleeping through the Christmas holidays in Winznau Marsh – something had to be done! The only thing that put me off now was the thought of finding a room in Zurich. I'd probably have to do without a flat of my own, and live in lodgings.

Then it occurred to me that, in the summer, Claudia had talked about going to Germany for a semester or two, to Kiel or Hamburg, as a counterpart to Heinrich's stay in Zurich. If she really did go, there would be a free room in the house in Zweierstrasse, at least for the beginning.

The last time I'd seen Claudia had been here in the Marsh, the Sunday Monica brought her and Heinrich along to lunch. The walk on the dam along the canal to Obergösgen and then back through the wilderness along the bank of the Old Aare, it must have been the end of August or the beginning of September. The relapse with Ruth and the subsequent break-up with Monica had made it impossible for me to keep in contact with Claudia.

I waited until the New Year, kept putting off phoning her.

No, she said, nothing was likely to come of the semester abroad. She wanted to get the next exam behind her as quickly as possible.

When I asked about Heinrich she answered evasively. They'd quarrelled. I didn't ask for details, only said that things were sure to sort themselves out.

I couldn't think of an excuse to go and see her.

And then I landed up in the kitchen in the Zweierstrasse after all. Without an excuse, I simply went along on a Friday in the middle of January, early in the evening.

We chatted for two hours across the round kitchen table, in public, as the Danish woman was drinking coffee with us. Afterwards, the chemistry student cooked leek rice and invited us all to join him in his meal. Claudia opened a bottle of red wine.

After the washing-up had been done, the two others went back to their rooms. Claudia and I remained alone in the kitchen.

We couldn't avoid talking about Heinrich any longer.

He was supposed to come to Switzerland between Christmas and New Year, she said. They'd planned to go skiing in the Engadine with a couple of student friends, everything had been settled, accommodation for a week's stay had already been booked. But in the middle of December he phoned her. Quite unexpectedly he'd been offered a trainee job at the university hospital, the professor for whom he was writing his thesis had drawn his attention to it, he hadn't been able to say no. Couldn't they postpone the skiing holiday? There was bound still to be snow in the Alps in March.

Perhaps she'd said something wrong to start with. But it wasn't the first time he'd changed his mind like that, so suddenly, and more or less at the last moment.

He'd said she should come to Kiel in the Christmas holidays. After all, he wouldn't be on duty at the hospital all the time. Kiel in the winter also had its charms, she'd see what it was like there in winter.

Maybe she'd said the wrong thing again. In any case Heinrich was offended. Clearly he'd expected her to agree to his suggestion without further ado.

He'd written her a long letter in which he accused her of not showing enough understanding with regard to the optimal advancement of his studies – those were his words, 'optimal advancement of studies' – and that she didn't recognise the importance of such trainee jobs, and how rare such opportunities were for him. In short, he'd proven that she was wrong in every respect.

They'd often quarrelled here in Zweierstrasse, she said, but it had never been really serious, at least it had never become really serious. But now, the quarrelling on the phone and in the letters had somehow got out of hand.

She hadn't gone to Kiel. And she hadn't gone on a skiing holiday either.

We were sitting at the round kitchen table. At first she talked hesitantly, but she didn't stop talking.

Heinrich was dreadfully ambitious, she said. He always had to be the best. He'd inherited that from his father, a former physics student who'd had to break off his studies due to the war and then, as a village schoolmaster, had transferred his ambitions to his son. And Heinrich was happy to take them on.

The flat countryside up there by the sea was beautiful, she said. They'd gone on excursions almost every day in Heinrich's father's car. To Brunsbüttel and to the village where his father had had his first job after the war and where Heinrich had grown up. To Itzehoe, Heide, right up to Husum.

The dykes stretching into the distance. Grazing cows. Clear views across fields. Lighthouses, breakwaters, fishing cutters, dockside bars, high tide and low tide, wind force, raspberry bushes, last spring's floods, seaside hotels, district hospitals. Seen from Switzerland, it was the other end of the world, and she'd liked it.

A minute of silence for Heinrich.

Then Claudia asked about Monica. I told her the story with Monica, part of it; I told her the Ruth story, part of it; I admitted I'd behaved shabbily.

Confessions so easily made were not worth much, said Claudia. It had been a mean thing to do, I said, and seeing that for what it was, and admitting it to myself – even that had been no easy thing for me. She didn't believe me. I elaborated: how the beginning with Monica had been the beginning of the end and how a person named Claudia had played the main role, in the beginning, in the end, all the time.

'You could have replaced any of them, but nobody could replace you.'

'You're crazy,' she said.

'If you say so, it must be true.'

A minute of silence for the Claudia of those days. Now she was embarrassed, but not overly so.

She made me feel dissatisfied with myself, I said. Not that that was to be regretted, on the contrary, it was to be welcomed. I was lazy and sleepy, but when I was with her I woke up, at least for a while. Instantly I'd feel a desire for change and make all kinds of good resolutions. Even my teaching benefited.

'It would certainly have been better,' I said, 'if I'd already told you something like that in the spring. But I couldn't. And now it looks as if I'd only been waiting for Heinrich to be gone, for him to be back in Germany.'

'He's been away ever since October, unfortunately,' she said.

'Of course I'd have made a fool of myself,' I said, 'but on the other hand I wouldn't be standing here now as though I'd been waiting all along – in ambush, so to speak – for a quarrel to break out between the two of you. For that's what it looks like now. But it's not like that, it really isn't.'

'What is it like then?'

'Doubly awful. I wasn't waiting for anything, anything at all. You and Heinrich, it was evident, so obvious– as it still is. As far as our – no, sorry, I mean as far as my – old story is concerned, what's over is over. But there's still some attachment, I don't deny it, and if I said anything else you wouldn't believe me anyway. But I wasn't waiting or hoping for things to be over between you and Heinrich, really I wasn't.'

'I don't know,' she said.

'Do you think I do?'

The stove was overheated with briquettes, the balcony door a few centimetres open. Claudia soon fell asleep. Streaks of light moved across the wall and across the ceiling whenever a car passed by down in the street. There hadn't been any trams for a long time. Wide awake, on the very edge of the bed; sweating with freezing cold feet.

Once, it was getting on for four o'clock, she turned away from the wall and I thought she was waking up. Then she only put her arm around me, snuggled up closer. I heard her steady breathing, felt the light pressure of her arm, now and then I felt a twitching, I didn't move.

She'd set the alarm and got up with me. She accompanied me to the railway station. Snow was falling. I remember the black water of the Sihl river. At the station buffet we had a cup of coffee together.

The early train to Olten. I'd have just enough time to pick up my already packed briefcase in Winznau Marsh. And if there wasn't enough time, I'd go straight to school without the briefcase and my preparations. It wouldn't be the first time I'd had to go to school without having been back home properly beforehand.

In any case, I wouldn't be teaching much longer.

That Saturday morning I stood absent-mindedly in front of the class and everything went well.

On Sunday I phoned Zurich. The Danish woman said Claudia had already gone home yesterday.

I rang her there.

We met in Olten. She had to change trains anyway.

Such happiness! And it had only come about thanks to a series of coincidences. It was a coincidence that I'd met her and Heinrich in the Nord-Süd cinema; a coincidence that, just that once, Monica who happened to live near Zweierstrasse had been with me; a coincidence that the two women got on well with each another; and the fortuitous fact that Heinrich's father was a village schoolteacher made it easy for me to converse naturally with Heinrich.

A succession of minor things, one thing combining with the other, as if there was nothing special about it. Indeed, there was nothing special about it. That old story's been completely forgotten, no one thinks of it any more! Heinrich was right for Claudia, and Claudia was right for him, I saw that with equanimity, yes even with relief. There was no need to undertake anything, no need for deliberation, no need for daring, it wouldn't end in an attack, it wouldn't end in an affair.

We went to the cinema together.

Kubrik's *Dr Strangelove or: How I Learned to Stop Worrying and Love the Bomb*. Claudia also liked the film, we had a long discussion about it in the Bodega in the Niederdorf.

After the film *The Loneliness of the Long Distance Runner* we quarrelled. Tom Courtenay plays a working-class boy in a borstal who is offered early release from the institution provided he wins a marathon for the home. The governor of the borstal gives him permission to train every morning in the environs of the institution. On those long, early morning runs he recalls scenes from the life that has taken him here. He didn't do anything really bad: small thefts, more tests of courage than criminal acts. But he is the child of a working-class family, so they didn't hesitate to crack down on him. Something like that could have happened to me too, if I hadn't fallen into my model pupil role; and my sister Katherine had got pretty close to having it happen to her. Finally, the young delinquent doesn't win the marathon after all, he loses the race on purpose in order to spite the borstal governor, who only wants to improve his own image with his pupil's victory. I was moved by the film, more than I cared to admit. But it left Claudia cold; she found the film interesting, that was all.

On the other hand she felt a lot of sympathy for beautiful Monica Vitti in *Il Deserto Rosso*.

Then again, we both liked Pasolini's *Il Vangelo secondo Matteo*. And since then I've never missed an opportunity to see the film again, either as a rerun or on television.

Once we went to a concert in the Tonhalle together. Once we went on a walk up the Uetliberg. And one Saturday we went on a pub crawl through the Niederdorf when 'immigrants' from the Catholic cantons of central Switzerland were celebrating their Carnival.

If I'd have had my way I'd have gone to Zurich every day.

Claudia had an exam that spring and was already preparing for it, and nearly every time we talked about anything connected with the university and her studies she would start talking about Heinrich. Or she so obviously avoided all mention of Heinrich that, for that very reason, he secretly became part of the conversation. I noticed, and she noticed that I'd noticed.

It didn't worry me that Claudia thought about Heinrich on such occasions, in fact it moved me that she should be talking about him with me of all people. Being a stopgap wasn't all that bad.

The way she'd stubbornly defend some theory or other. The way she, who was normally so aloof, would sometimes listen ingenuously like a child. The way she'd drop down on her front, burrowing her head next to mine in the checkered pillows, her hip bones, her collarbones, her shoulder blades and all her ribs and all the bones of her spine.

Stop it, stop it!

A slight feeling of triumph, that was probably part of it too. Got there after all! He who laughs last. And that it had happened so simply, almost as a matter of course!

Claudia regretted nothing. However, the difference between Heinrich and me became apparent, and not to my advantage. Even though she never said anything of the sort, it was something I sensed.

We might have grown close in time. Get to know each other in little things, build up from there, as the sensible and modest saying goes. Did I really exert myself? But exerting myself would hardly have got me anywhere.

'Listen, you're a nice chap, and I know very well that you tried very hard back then. But I still didn't really fall for you. I didn't chase after Heinrich. And I'm not chasing after you, in case that's what you thought.'

Yet all I'd done was mention Ruth, nothing else. All I said was that I'd run into her at the station in Olten. She was dressed very elegantly and had caught my eye on the opposite platform. She'd been on the way to a concert in Basel and she'd had time for a cup of coffee.

And that did it. No, it wasn't that Claudia was jealous, certainly not.

This time too there was a sequel in written form. Not a trilogy, Heaven forbid! I wrote her a letter. I composed it as I walked along the canal.

She rang me.

Perhaps I was right. But that didn't change anything. Much as she regretted it, she couldn't be the person I imagined.

I asked how she'd got on in the exams. I apologised again for being a nuisance.

She demurred: it won't have done anyone any harm.

There was nothing to add to that.

It's not as though I'd eyed Erica long before as a possible almost-girlfriend, a girlfriend in reserve. But I'd known her for quite some time: she'd been appointed as a secondary school teacher in Trimbach, which meant that she also became the inspector of the primary school in Winznau.

It was my first winter there. Ruth was visiting me regularly in Winznau Marsh and, what with all the concerts she took me to, the weekly trips to Zurich where I attended lectures and often met Bede and occasionally also Monica – what with all those distractions I barely noticed my new inspector. And especially during that muddle with Ruth and Monica, and then the relapse with Claudia – I certainly had no eyes for her then.

She'd made her first official visit to the Winznau school in Advent. On the last day before the Christmas holidays my two classes were to perform a nativity play, and all the other classes and the parents had been invited. And since there was no room big enough either in the old or in the new school building, the play would be performed in the hall of the Trauben restaurant.

Erica caught me at a rehearsal. She praised the children's correct German pronunciation and asked me how that could be achieved with children. But she made fun of the naturalistic mise en scène. Were the bales of straw, the wheelbarrow as a crib, the flails and the paraffin lamps really necessary, she asked. The dry manner in which she gave her friendly criticism struck me even then.

No doubt it was rather reckless to be starting an affair with one's inspector. Risky for me? More likely for Erica. Ruth had always been careful to park her car a long way away from my flat. Erica, however, didn't think much of such hole and corner stuff. Straightforward and self-assured as she was, she didn't bother about what people said.

Perhaps that was what was special about it.

May Day in Olten. I was astonished to see my inspector in the parade. That's how the story began. And in spite of my initial hesitation, the story took its course, and some time or other I noticed that there was no need to look around for a replacement for this Erica. Did she latch on to me? Did I latch on to her? There was hardly any anxiety or apprehension involved. On the contrary, there was something calm, relaxed, almost self-evident about it.

Erica knew what she wanted. One of the things was to get married and have children. And strangely enough, she seemed to think someone like me was the right person for that. I was too surprised to resist.

Clearly it was neither a Clauditis attack nor was it an affair, it was something different. And even if it took me a while to realise it, in the end I did.

XI

THAT SUMMER – EPILOGUE

'So all that was going on and we never noticed … Good-by to clocks ticking … and Mama's sunflowers. And food and coffee. And new-ironed dresses and hot baths … and sleeping and waking up. Oh, earth, you're too wonderful for anybody to realize you.'

Thornton Wilder, *Our Town*

'That blood pressure business, forget it. You'll live to ninety with it.'

'Oh yes, and take a tablet every day till then. Besides, the question is: what condition will I be in when I'm eighty, not to speak of ninety? A few joint replacements, deaf, shaky and a head full of memory gaps.'

'Oh come on! You use your head every day, probably even more than I do. It's hardly likely that anything will happen.'

'But you don't know for sure.'

'Doctors never know anything for sure.'

'And say you're more or less all right in the head, once you're eighty no one takes you seriously any more. It's already started now, by the way. People are markedly polite and kind towards you, almost protective. In an increasingly professional way – much like you now.'

'Nonsense!'

'If you say so. But you must admit that you'd have spoken differently to a patient.'

'You mean I'd have been more professional, gentler?'

'Quite!'

Walden; or, Life in the Woods, Thoreau in the house he'd built for himself by Walden Pond near Concord. Be alone to start on something new? To slip out of your old skin?

When I left Oberdorf back then, it was definitely more than a whim. The whole of that summer had been a long farewell, and leaving home was only the end of it.

And those moves later on, each time it was a new beginning. Behind the mountain: the attic room with the kitchenette in the corridor. The small flat in Winznau Marsh. Then the big house right next to it. And also the narrow, high-ceilinged room in Bread Street in Edinburgh where I spent my two semesters abroad.

Nothing to do with women, nothing like that. But it's true that I did think that moving out of Winznau would change something.

Here's the pretext and the truism: We've lived too close to each other too long. A little distance can be a good thing.

It might just as well have been an allotment hut by the railway lines. Or else the 'Round Hole' up there on the mountain slope, or the 'Smugglers Cave' behind the quarry in the Klus Gorge, or a caravan on some remote camping site. The dream of the simple life – as though my life hadn't always been simple enough. To disappear for a couple of months and then turn up again. To be alone for a time and then mingle with people again. Is that why I moved here? Not male fantasy, simply a childhood dream?

Run, run! Why? To feel refreshed in the evening? To counter overweight, high blood pressure?

No, I don't run around in the morning. In the early morning I have other things to do, in the early morning I feel fresh without a run.

While I was working on my thesis, I used to run along the canal every evening, Winznau-Obergösgen return, a fit mind in a fit body. Later on however, once I was in my teaching routine, those spiritual exercises ceased.

So now I go running again. In the late afternoon I do a few rounds on the campus of the Kantonsschule. From the neglected hard pitch south of the science building along the cinder track to the gyms and Fegetz Avenue, then on the tarmac path back to the science building – six hundred metres, apparently. Always with a slight forward lean, as though I was about to let myself fall on my nose. In that way your legs move almost automatically. It's more letting yourself fall forward than proper running.

Quarter past five, a class is clearing hurdles and other apparatus from the hard pitch. Gasser, a former colleague at the teacher training college, is standing by the stairs calling out something to the young people. I stop for a moment.

I ask how things are going and what's new. Whether he still teaches games at the university of applied sciences and arts.

No, only here. And he's glad about that.

If I'd kept on teaching to the end, I'd have stopped this summer, so by now I'd already have been in retirement for quite a few weeks.

Uncanny how quickly the weeks, the months, the years pass.

Gasser doesn't ask me about my Anderson book, probably he doesn't know anything about it. On retirement, I immediately got down to work on it, but with the feeling that I had plenty of time ahead, not only for Anderson, but also for Edgar Lee Masters and a few others before him, for Thornton Wilder and a few more after him. Winesburg and Grover's Corner and all the other small towns, together with their inhabitants, and Spoon River, Gopher Prairie, Monterey, Jefferson, Concord, Altamont, Ithaca et cetera.

At least I read a lot.

I already had drafts when I moved here, and I thought that with all that free time I'd be able to complete the work in such a way that it would include everything that it should.

And now, is everything in it?

Anna's Benno may be right to be so thorough, I too could go on reading and writing and rereading for years and years. But what of it? It's taken long enough already. Better to have two hundred pages in a definitive version than one thousand pages of draft material.

'Really? You once wrote a play? And the play still exists, I mean on paper, and it's lying around somewhere – hey, you must give it me, I want to read it.'

'And make fun of it, you'd enjoy that, wouldn't you?'

'Don't be so distrustful! I had no idea that you used to be interested in the theatre. In any event, you never took me to see a play, you often took us to the cinema, never to the theatre. You left that to Erica. And yet you've written a play yourself, that's cool, really! Come on, I'm going to read it.'

'No you won't.'

'Okay, then I'll just imagine all the terrible things that might be in it.'

'For example?'

'Murder and manslaughter and some gruesome family history. What do you think of that?'

'A run-of-the-mill family story, that would be more like it.'

'Well, will you let me read it?'

'Certainly not.'

That frightful trilogy! Even after years, I was overcome with uneasiness whenever I thought of those three plays. I preferred not to remember what I'd written, or the fact that I'd given the text to Claudia to read, I'd have liked nothing better than to forget it.

On the other hand I was not ashamed, either then or later, that I'd written something and that I'd stayed home for a couple of weeks to get on with it. I felt no shame at having lied to the teachers, or to my college friends, I wasn't ashamed of having got my father to sign all my cooked-up excuses. I'd done the right thing, I'd done what had to be done, including the lies, the half-lies, all the fibbing.

And it seemed to me that the more time passed, the more vivid that summer became. The escape to Zurich, the night in the allotments and the night by the lake, then the walks through the ripening wheat fields, the late morning walks, the walks in the afternoon, in the evening, the outer peace and the inner agitation. Paul Ganter, you were crazy once too, maybe not really completely mad, but slightly mad at least!

For a long time, I thought that it was my first love story that had got engraved in my mind, that had stayed in my memory in all its details. Indeed it was true that with each Clauditis attack, with each affair, the old story came back. No Maria or Madeleine, no Verena, Veronica,

Lina or Lena without Claudia. Whether it inhibited or advanced matters, confused or clarified the situation, the comparison with Claudia was always there.

It was still there with Erica, and only gradually faded away. Many other things now occupied my mind. I had to finish my studies as quickly as possible, and I had paternal duties. Then it was my teaching life again, later on the purchase of the house in Winznau, the conversion, the few additional jobs I hadn't been able to avoid taking on.

Until I suddenly noticed that, if anything at all from that time came to my mind, it was only those summer weeks that I remembered. And I recalled those summer weeks even without the hint of an attack or an affair that might have set me off. And I noticed that Claudia only came into it marginally, fleetingly, There was that slim girl, wasn't there? Who was the cause of it all. How on earth had it happened? And there I am again sitting on the landing beneath the lamp, my father stomps up the steps, glances over my shoulder and says: 'A play, my my, so late and still at it!' And I go on writing, no matter how hopeless, how pointless it is, that's precisely why I hang on, *Suddenly, Last Summer*, I'll get it behind me by going straight through the heart of it, and tomorrow I'll march through the Furrers' orchard again, walk along the Haselweg as far as the reservoir, turn left down to the wood; the serried stalks of wheat stand either side of the cart tracks all the way down to the shallow hollow, ears and ears of wheat, innumerable beneath the drifting shadows of summer clouds.

Sitting under the lamp at the small table out in the landing at night, and the walks through the fields – that's what kept coming to my mind, I don't know why. And even if I did, it wouldn't change anything. That strange state I was in during that strange summer, when I wrote and wrote, driven, drawn, permanently in fear of drying up. And suddenly I get going again, an idea turns up, I could just as well have had it three hours ago, nothing special, and with this one idea I can move on, not fleeing away from the thing, but fleeing through the very heart of the matter. And the small table under the lamp, the clothes on the coat hooks next to the kitchen door, the boarded floor, the shoe rack in the corner, the whole humble landing is the right setting for it.

But why, afterwards, did you recall that particular scene, that one and no other? What did it contain that moved you and made it meaningful for you? Was it the idea that, as long as you don't give up, as long as you remain focussed on a thing, as long as you don't stop working on it, as long as you don't run away, you'll find a solution, not the perfect one, not even a good solution, only something that will somehow help you move on?

Or am I looking in the wrong place? Might it not have been pure chance? For some reason I recall a scene a couple of weeks after it took place, it comes alive in my mind, it's present down to the last detail. And because I remembered it once, I easily remember it a second time, then a third and a fourth. The simple mechanism of repetition turns the random scene into a scene that stands out, and the oftener that late hour on the landing comes to mind in the following months and years, the more it looks as if there was something remarkable about it.

All along I'd been keenly aware of how little time I had left, four weeks, another three, only two weeks left now; and yet, despite the stress, single days and nights passed by in a blur. Exhausted, I'd fall asleep, to wake in dull fatigue; I was running out of days and yet time still seemed to be standing still. Being fraught with diligence was something I knew well, but previously the stress had always been reasonable, limited, almost sedate; now I was running on ahead, running and running, and in spite of the confinement I felt almost inebriated.

What became of them? Close acquaintances became distant acquaintances, and as regards some of them, I don't even know if they're still alive.

Monica has been retired for a while, after all she's five years older than me. Occasionally we send each other picture postcards, or a short letter at New Year, sometimes I forget, sometimes she's the one who forgets.

And Ruth the organ player? I haven't a clue, I never heard anything from her any more.

And Jacob? After studying at the music academy, he became a répétiteur and opera choirmaster somewhere in Germany. Later he organised all kinds of events in the French-speaking part of Switzerland.

Bede had a great academic career, though not in philosophy. After his PhD, he worked as a German teacher in Olten, and wrote reviews for the *Neue Zürcher Zeitung* as a sideline. In those days we occasionally met.

But by the time I got a job at the Kantonsschule Olten myself, he'd already left. He'd qualified as a university lecturer early on, and had been given a teaching assignment at the University of Dortmund. Later, he moved from Dortmund to the University of Education in Freiburg im Breisgau. Apparently his special topic for a while was literature for children and young adults: *Robinson Crusoe, Treasure Island,* the *Leatherstocking Tales* et cetera as adapted for children and young adults.

Corinne worked as a stewardess for Swissair after her Matura. She married a banker, and still lives in Küsnacht on Lake Zurich. Her garden is said to be renowned among rose experts.

And Elizabeth? Killed in an avalanche during a skiing tour in the Bernese Oberland. It's the saddest story, probably also the stupidest. Although I only heard about it years later, it hit me hard and made me depressed for weeks. As if I'd always owed Elizabeth something, and now I could never make amends. Claudia's best friend, I really should have noticed her at some point even then, the clever girl, her bright face with the clear features, the firm mouth and grey eyes, her straight shoulders. She was a head taller than Claudia, a tall girl with a great mop of hair, a contrast to delicate, sinewy, boney, almost angular Claudia. Not that I didn't have an eye for such things, I'd seen them all right, I just hadn't been fully aware. And stupid creature that I was, I'd felt so relieved when I finally noticed that that lovely girl was going out with Bede, and that Bede had invited Elizabeth and not Claudia to the Dornachia fraternity dance, although he and Jacob could be seen at least twice a week at the Carrels' house.

I never saw through that kind of thing in time. Not an innocent from the countryside, just a country bumpkin. And with such a feeble understanding of amorous matters I thought I could write a play!

And the Carrels' house?

No, I never went and took another look at it this time round. I'll leave it standing down there on the Aare as it appears in my memory, down there on the Aare, with the extension, the roof terrace, the fence, the bushes, the alder and the ash trees. There are no Carrels living there any more. When I once happened to meet Claudia at a vernissage at the art museum in Olten – it must have been ten or more years ago – she told me that her parents now lived in Lausanne.

'So you're moving out? Is that final?' asks Anna.

'The Portmanns need the flat themselves. Their nephew's been working for Ypsomed since last autumn, he lives in Baden, the commute is too long for him.'

'So it's back to Winznau? Does Erica know?'

'We've discussed it.'

'And, are you welcome?'

'I don't know. I suppose so.'

'What a strange couple you are!'

'What's so strange? There can only be two reasons for me not to return to Winznau. Firstly the mess upstairs, the three rooms still chock-a-block with school stuff. And secondly all the social obligations. Erica will want to invite someone to a meal every week, she did that without me too, but as soon as I'm back home I won't be able to hide away upstairs, will I?'

'Is that your only problem? If you're not careful you'll land up with all kinds of eccentric habits in your old age. Hardly ever tidying up, unable to throw anything away and, on top of that, avoiding company, it's a syndrome, the syndrome has a name, and the prognosis is bad.'

She laughed as she said it. It's unlikely things will get as bad as all that.

Today, coming from town through Loreto Meadows in the grey, early dusk, I suddenly remember the combine harvester I saw driving round the field here last summer. That was six months ago, and yet it seems no more than two or three weeks. Only just recently, the red combine harvester was drawing tracks round and round the wheatfield here. On my way home I'd stopped and stood here to watch the droning, dust-spraying machine.

THE AUTHOR

www.erhard-von-bueren.ch

Erhard von Büren was born near Solothurn, Switzerland. After a PhD in Psychology and German philology from Zurich University and study stays in France he worked as a teacher in advanced teacher training.

Besides various articles in anthologies and journals, he has had three novels published in Switzerland: *Abdankung. Ein Bericht* (Zytglogge Verlag, Bern 1989), *Wespenzeit* (Rotpunktverlag, Zurich 2000), *Ein langer blauer Montag* (verlag die Brotsuppe. Biel/Bienne 2013).

After *Epitaph for a Working Man* and *Wasp Days*, *A Long Blue Monday* is the third of his books to be published in English.

Erhard von Büren has won various literary awards including the Canton of Solothurn Prize for Literature in 2007. He lives in Solothurn.

THE TRANSLATOR

Helen Wallimann was born and brought up in the UK. After her MA from Edinburgh University she worked in publishing in Munich, Paris and London. From 1973 to 2001 she was employed as a teacher of French and English at the Kantonsschule Solothurn. She taught English at Chinese universities for two years.

Literary translations that have been published in book form include: *Legends from the Swiss Alps.* MCCM creations, Hong Kong 2009 (trans. from German); Leung Ping-kwan, *The Visible and the Invisible. Poems.* MCCM creations, Hong Kong 2012 (trans. from Chinese); Erhard von Büren, *Epitaph for a Working Man.* Matador 2015; *Wasp Days.* Matador 2016.

(The author and the translator can both be found on *facebook*.)

Epitaph for a Working Man

Erhard von Büren's laconic tale
of a life and a death

How earthy ... is the old man's behaviour, are his
repartees and the monologues which Erhard von Büren
has picked up with a sure touch and converted into
authentic spoken language. *Neue Zürcher Zeitung*

A novel to get you thinking. *Amazon customer*

There is real warmth and heart to these characters which
makes them hard to leave. *Bookmuse*

This moving portrayal of the last days of an old man
packs a powerful emotional punch. I loved this book
and found it touching and engaging, with excellent
characterisation and authentic dialogue. *Goodreads*

WASP DAYS

Erhard von Büren's ironic but amiable look at life in all its diversity makes for an enjoyable and intellectually stimulating read

A book that creates the kind of sweltry summer lethargy in which you simply abandon yourself to the quiet flow of words. *Mittelland Zeitung*

It is a pleasure to follow the author on his wanderings through the multifaceted world of his thoughts. *Neue Zürcher Zeitung*

The story of an ordinary person with a fairly ordinary life, when told with humour, with a certain amount of detachment and with intelligence, can often produce a first-class novel as it has done in this case. *The Modern Novel*